AF440133

THE WATCHER

The Watcher

CAROL A CAMPBELL

To My Mom and Dad

Here's To Chasing Dreams &
Finding My Way Back Home!

The Watcher
Copyright © 2024 by Carol Campbell
All rights reserved. No part of this book may be reproduced
in any manner whatsoever without written permission except
in the case of brief quotations embodied in critical articles and
reviews.
First Printing, 2024

Prologue

Christmas in Bayou Vista was the heart of Southern charm. Every December, the town square came alive with twinkling lights, music, and the warm laughter of families. This year, the festivities carried a renewed spark, as if everyone was eager to shake off a dark year. Rumors of a killer hiding in the Devil's Marsh had finally quieted, and folks felt ready to move on. The Sheriff had even tucked away those unsolved cases, giving people the feeling they could breathe easy again.

Main Street was a picture-perfect holiday scene. Shops glowed with warmth, each decorated in wreaths and garlands. At *Frog's Delight Bakery*, gingerbread houses and frosted cakes filled the window display, watched over by a grinning frog statue in a Santa hat. A few doors down, *Bayou Bliss Coffee Shop* was wrapped in fairy lights, with Brenda Menifee behind the counter, serving up spiced lattes and peppermint mochas that filled the air with holiday scents.

Cindy's boutique, *Burning Love*, had railings wrapped in red and gold lights, and *Taylor's Treasure*, the new gift shop, stood out with silver and blue garlands and a little Christmas tree decorated by local artists. In the center of the square, a towering Christmas tree sparkled with ornaments brought by every family in town. Each one held a memory, a piece of the town's history, and by nightfall, folks gathered around it, sipping cider and sharing stories.

Across the square, *Pearls & Crystal Cove*, the jewelry shop run by Gail, Patricia, and Margie, had a touch of elegance with pearl-studded wreaths and strings of crystals. Meanwhile, Loretta, Tricia, and Jill were busy at *Heavenly Wishes*, gathering toys and food for underprivileged families, filling crates with gifts they'd pass out later in the week. This season, for Bayou Vista, was about more than decorations—it was about coming together and looking out for each other.

At *Bayou Belle Beauty*, the air smelled of hair sprays and shampoos as folks streamed in, looking their best for holiday gatherings. *C&D Kwik Stop*, the reliable corner store, was decked in candy cane lights, with Dondi and Cindy running a holiday special on eggnog and stocking stuffers. Even *Shanster Travels* had joined in the fun, windows decked out in tinsel and travel-themed ornaments, offering deals to those dreaming of a white Christmas.

Just down the street, Firecracker, known for her fiery personality, held court as the bakery manager at *Berry's Market*. She was busy stocking the bakery shelves with all the Christmas essentials, chatting up customers, and sending them off with a hearty "Merry Christmas, darlin'!" as they bustled around, gathering treats and groceries for their family dinners. To Firecracker, there was no holiday too small for her enthusiasm—and she made sure everyone left with a little extra cheer.

As evening set in, *Tanya's Crawfish*, a local favorite, filled up with people looking to warm up with gumbo and enjoy the season. At the edge of town, *Jason's Bar* was alive with holiday lights strung along the bar, and Jason himself was serving up festive drinks to folks toasting to brighter days.

From his shop, Micky Vermooch of *Micky's Magical Things* watched it all. He'd decorated his window with a wreath of herbs and hung enchanted candles that flickered warmly. He waved at neighbors passing by, nodding at the kids racing past, faces bright with excitement. He wanted to join fully, but held onto a quiet truth: he knew the real threat hadn't passed. Evil didn't just vanish—it lurked just beyond the glow of the season's cheer.

Micky kept that knowledge to himself. After all, it was Christmas. Folks had waited so long for peace, and he'd be darned if he'd spoil it with worry. As kids played by the tree and couples strolled hand-in-hand, he let himself get caught up in the cheer.

Inside *Bayou Bliss*, Brenda called out, "Merry Christmas!" to each customer as the door chimed open, letting in cool night air. She poured her heart into every cup, from peppermint mochas to cinnamon lattes, each sip carrying a bit of holiday joy.

The weather was a perfect Southern chill, fifty degrees during the day and dipping into the thirties by night. Folks huddled closer around the Christmas tree, sharing stories and laughs. Even Catrina from *Catrina's Closet* stepped out to chat with friends, adjusting the sparkling outfits in her window display. The holiday spirit filled every corner, from Taylor's handcrafted ornaments to the gingerbread drifting from Frog's Delight.

On the edge of the square, *St. Theresa's Church* stood, softly lit with white lights. Preacher John had arranged a nativity scene on the lawn, each figure delicately dusted with frost. The banner over the door read, "Peace on Earth, Good Will Toward Men," a message Bayou Vista clung to. To them, this was more than just decoration—it was a prayer for brighter days.

As the evening wore on, Loretta, Tricia, and Jill moved around the square, laughing and gathering donations. Their smiles warmed everyone they met, spreading hope and light. For them, it was about bringing joy to families who'd had a rough year.

Micky watched from his doorway, his heart heavy with pride and sorrow. He knew there was a killer out there, somewhere beyond the lights, but he kept that truth locked away. This holiday season was about letting folks celebrate, letting them believe that, for once, all was well.

As the last carol ended and families drifted home, Micky took one last look around. The lights flickered in the cool air, the giant Christmas tree casting a warm glow. Folks lingered, hands full of gifts, hearts full of peace. It felt like a fresh start, a new chapter.

But as he turned to lock up, a shiver ran through him. The square had grown quiet, almost too still. There was a chill in the air that wasn't from the temperature, something that slipped into the empty spaces, hiding in the corners.

He looked back at the silent square, the lights casting long shadows across empty streets. For now, everyone believed the worst was behind them. But Micky knew that peace could be as fleeting as a candle in the wind, and that sometimes, things came back, biding their time.

In the quiet stillness of the town square, something lingered just out of sight, like a whisper waiting to be heard. Though Micky couldn't see it, he felt it—a watchful gaze, an unspoken promise in the winter air.

Christmas in Bayou Vista had brought light and laughter. But somewhere, in the shadowed edges of town, something waited, patient and unseen. And the people of Bayou Vista had no idea what was coming.

~ 1 ~

STRANGE ARRIVAL

December swept into Bayou Vista like an old friend, carrying with it the kind of crisp, bracing chill that made the town feel alive. Folks were up early, stringing Christmas lights on their porches and hanging wreaths on their doors. Over at *Bayou Bliss Coffee Shop,* Brenda Menifee was already setting up for the morning rush, her red and black apron tied neatly around her waist. The place smelled of fresh-brewed coffee and cinnamon, with a hint of peppermint drifting from the festive holiday drinks she'd prepared. Red and gold fairy lights twinkled along the windows, casting a warm glow that softened the edges of the early morning shadows.

Inside, a group of women had gathered around their usual table, their voices rising and falling like a soft hum. Patricia, Margie, and Gail were there, laughing and chatting, each of them clutching warm cups of spiced lattes or black coffee. Tricia and Jill joined them not long after, sliding their chairs close to the group, eager to join the morning's talk.

"Oh, honey," Gail sighed, taking a sip from her mug, "I swear, this year's felt like five rolled into one. We could all use a break."

"Well, at least it's Christmas," Brenda said, flashing a grin as she wiped down the counter. "And as far as I'm concerned, if we can survive the past few years, we can survive just about anything."

The women chuckled, nodding in agreement. As they swapped stories and the occasional recipe, the shop door opened with a jingle, and in walked Sheriff Emmett Johnson, a tall man with a muscular build, his uniform dusted with mud from the bayou. He tipped his hat to the ladies and made his way to a table in the corner, where Micky Vermooch and Preacher John were already seated.

Micky looked up with a half-smile, his eyes twinkling beneath his thick, gray wool cap. He wore a scarf with mystical symbols embroidered on it, a signature look that added to his quiet mystery. Preacher John gave the Sheriff a nod, and Sheriff Emmett eased himself into a chair, stretching his long legs.

"Sheriff," Micky greeted him, raising his coffee in a small toast. "Morning. How are things out there?"

Emmett shrugged, rubbing a hand over his jaw. "Quiet for now, but you never know. Got a fisherman down at the docks with a story that'll make the hair on your neck stand up."

As if on cue, the door jingled again, and in came Hank Mullins, the fisherman. Hank was a burly man in his sixties with skin bronzed by years spent on the water. His face was lined, his hands rough and calloused, and he walked with a bit of a limp from an old injury he never talked about. His cap was pulled low over his forehead, and his jacket smelled faintly of salt and mud.

"Hank," Sheriff Emmett called, waving him over. "You got Brenda here fussin' over you?"

Hank tipped his cap at the ladies, who gave him curious nods and grins. He shuffled over to the counter where Brenda had already poured him a hot cup of black coffee.

"Thanks, Brenda. You're a saint," Hank muttered, nodding his thanks before joining the Sheriff and the others at their table.

The Sheriff leaned back, giving Hank a piercing gaze. "You wanna tell us what you saw this morning?"

Hank glanced around, lowering his voice as though he were afraid someone outside might hear.

"Was out near the marsh, you know, checkin' traps and mindin' my own. But just as I was gettin' ready to pack up, I saw... someone. Or somethin'."

The table fell silent, and even the ladies nearby paused their chatter to listen in.

"Go on," Preacher John said gently, leaning forward with a worried frown.

Hank swallowed, eyes darting around the room. "It was a figure, cloaked all in black, just standin' there at the edge of the marsh...a little past Preacher's Pond. Watchin'. Couldn't see a face or nothin'. Just... there, like they were waitin' for somethin'."

Sheriff Emmett's brow furrowed. "And you sure it wasn't someone just wandering out there? Maybe a lost tourist or someone camping nearby?"

"No, sir," Hank replied, shaking his head. "I know these marshes like the back of my hand. Ain't no one supposed to be out there, and sure as hell no one I recognize."

Micky took a slow sip of his coffee, his eyes never leaving Hank. "Did they say anything? Did they notice you?"

Hank hesitated, his fingers tightening around his coffee mug. "Don't know if they saw me, but I got the feelin' they did. It was like... well, like they knew I was there, but didn't care none. Just went back to lookin' out over the marsh, still as stone."

The room grew quiet, everyone's eyes fixed on Hank. Even the women at the other table had gone still, their usual gossip forgotten in the face of this unsettling tale.

Gail leaned in closer to her friends, whispering, "Lord have mercy. Do you think it could be that old ghost story folks used to tell?"

"Oh, don't start with that nonsense," Margie replied, shivering slightly. "Probably just some wanderer looking for trouble."

But Patricia shook her head. "Nothing about this town has ever been simple. I'd believe Hank before I'd brush it off as a tourist."

The Sheriff cleared his throat, bringing the attention back to the table. "Alright, Hank. Appreciate you telling me. I'll go take a look later today, see if there's any tracks or signs of someone passing through."

Hank just nodded, sipping his coffee and glancing out the window, as though expecting to see that figure standing there, watching.

Outside, Bayou Vista bustled on, unaware of the growing unease inside the coffee shop. The Christmas lights sparkled on every corner, and the laughter of children echoed down the street. Folks shuffled between shops, admiring decorations and picking up last-minute gifts. Brenda kept the coffee coming, her voice bright as she wished each customer a Merry Christmas, but the tension at Micky's table was thick.

"Well," Preacher John said finally, breaking the silence, "maybe it's just one of those strange things that happen sometimes. Folks get spooked easy this time of year, what with the long nights and all."

Micky, however, looked thoughtful. "There's more to this town than meets the eye, especially Devil's Marsh, and you all know it as well as I do. Something's out there, even if we can't quite see it yet."

As if to change the subject, Sheriff Emmett glanced over to the ladies. "Alright, what's the latest news? Y'all always have the good stories."

Patricia smirked, folding her arms. "You mean the gossip, Sheriff?"

"Don't know what you mean by that," he replied with a grin. "Just keeping up with the town, is all."

Gail laughed, nudging Margie. "Well, we heard *Taylor's Treasure* might be getting a surprise visit from an inspector next week. And I wouldn't be shocked if Catrina from *Catrina's Closet* had something to do with it—she's been eyeing Taylor's shop since it opened."

"Oh, Lord, here we go," Margie chuckled. "This town's got more stories than the Bible."

Preacher John just chuckled, settling back in his chair, while Micky's eyes sparkled with quiet amusement, taking in the warmth and camaraderie with a touch of nostalgia.

But as Sheriff Emmett looked out the window, his gaze drifted toward the edge of town, where Hank had described that cloaked figure. Despite the laughter and holiday cheer, a chill settled over him, the memory of Hank's words lingering. Bayou Vista might have been dressed up in lights and wreaths, but there were shadows lurking in the cracks, just waiting to seep back in.

As the morning wore on, the coffee shop gradually filled with more folks stopping in, exchanging stories, laughs, and holiday cheer. But beneath it all, a whisper of unease lingered—a strange arrival, an unseen presence, a hint of something waiting just beyond the glow of Christmas. And for the first time that season, the festive warmth of Bayou Vista felt just a little colder.

~ 2 ~

ON THE FIRST NIGHT...

December 13th arrived in Bayou Vista with a soft mist hanging over the town, making the Christmas lights shimmer in a hazy glow. The morning started like any other, with folks stopping in for their usual coffees at *Bayou Bliss*, talking about holiday plans and wondering if there'd be any snow—unlikely as always, but it didn't stop them from hoping. The town had a coziness that day, a quiet kind of joy that only seemed to settle in once December rolled around.

But on the steps of a small house just outside the main square, an odd little package sat waiting, tied up in brown paper and twine. Matilda Sharbino, the town's *school bus driver*, nearly tripped over it when she came out to check the weather. She muttered under her breath as she looked down at it, her brow furrowing. Matilda wasn't one for surprises, and she sure wasn't expecting a package, especially one that looked like it'd come out of another era.

Picking it up carefully, she noticed a small note attached, just a scrap of paper tucked beneath the twine, handwritten in a spidery scrawl. "On the first night..." it read. The words made her uneasy, though she couldn't quite place why. She glanced around, but the street was still empty, the town barely stirring. With a sigh, she took the package inside, figuring it was just some kid playing a prank.

Inside, she set it on her table, untying the twine with a mix of curiosity and irritation. The brown paper fell away, revealing a small, tarnished locket. It was old, the kind of thing you'd find in an antique shop or maybe tucked away in a grandmother's jewelry box. Matilda turned it over in her hands, feeling the weight of it, the slight grit on its surface. There was something familiar about it, like she'd seen it before but couldn't quite remember where. She brushed off the feeling and set it aside, chalking it up to some odd holiday joke.

Meanwhile, in town, the usual crowd gathered at *Bayou Bliss*. Cindy Blevins from *Burning Love* had claimed her corner seat, her bright red scarf draped over her shoulders as she sipped her coffee and read from a magazine. She looked up as Loretta entered, giving her a warm wave.

"Loretta! Come sit, girl!" Cindy called, pulling out a chair with her free hand.

Loretta smiled and slid into the seat, setting her purse down. "Morning, Cindy. Ain't it just the busiest time of year?"

"Tell me about it," Cindy replied, rolling her eyes. "Been up to my ears in customers. Seems like everyone in town needs a little something special this Christmas."

"That's 'cause you got the hottest shop in Bayou Vista," Loretta teased, nudging her.

They shared a laugh, and just then, the door swung open, and in walked Jason, the owner of *Jason's Bar*, along with the *Mayor*, Steve Strittmatter. Jason gave a nod to Cindy and Loretta before making his way to the counter. He was a tall, broad-shouldered man with a gruff look that softened when he smiled.

"Hey there, Brenda!" he called to the woman behind the counter. "You got any of that peppermint coffee left?"

Brenda grinned and reached for a mug. "For you, Jason, I always got some. And you too, Steve?"

The Mayor chuckled, patting his stomach. "Just a regular for me, Brenda. I'm trying to fit into my Sunday suit for the holiday service."

Loretta and Cindy shared a smirk. The Mayor was always making the rounds, keeping up appearances, but they knew him well enough to see through the polished front.

As they all settled in, Sheriff Emmett entered, shaking off the chill from outside. He joined Jason and Steve, pulling his chair up to their table. "Morning, folks. What's all the chatter about?"

Jason leaned back, crossing his arms. "Nothing much. Just hearing the Mayor's diet."

The Sheriff chuckled warmly, tipping his hat. "Loretta, I can't thank you enough. Folks all over town are talking about the gifts you've delivered; you're bringing them a little Christmas light and easing some of their worries."

Loretta smiled. "Just doing my part, Sheriff. There's still plenty more to do."

The Sheriff chuckled warmly, tipping his hat. "With you around, Bayou Vista's in good hands."

Micky walked in just then, his thick, knitted cap pulled low over his brow, his scarf tucked around his neck in that way only he could pull off. With his English accent, he added a touch of the exotic to the place, and folks were always eager to hear his thoughts, especially on days like these when the mist still clung to the ground, giving the town an otherworldly feel.

"Good morning to you all," Micky greeted with a nod, settling himself at the counter with a warm smile. "Sheriff, Jason, Mayor Steve, and ladies," he added, acknowledging Cindy and Loretta with a small raise of his coffee cup once Brenda served him.

"Micky, you're looking mighty cheerful this morning," Cindy commented, grinning over her mug.

He chuckled softly. "Why not? It's Christmas, isn't it? Can't be walking around with a sour face this time of year. But I'll admit," he leaned in a bit, voice lowering, "something about the mist today felt... off."

They all glanced at him, a mix of curiosity and amusement on their faces. Loretta raised a brow. "You're not one for superstitions, are ya, Micky?"

He shrugged, a twinkle in his eye. "Well, maybe just a little. Never hurts to keep an open mind."

At that moment, the shop's bell rang again, and in walked Taylor, the owner of the new gift shop. She was dressed in a cozy green sweater and had a box of ornaments under her arm. Her eyes lit up when she saw the group.

"Y'all mind if I join?" she asked, pulling up a chair.

"Of course, darlin'," Cindy replied, scooting over. "You bringing us presents?"

Taylor laughed, setting the box down on the table. "Just some samples for the shop. Thought I'd see if anyone wanted one before they're all gone."

They rummaged through the box, admiring the ornaments—each one handmade, delicate, and painted with little holiday scenes. As they admired Taylor's creations, the conversation drifted to holiday plans, the tree lighting ceremony, and the big Christmas Eve service at St. Theresa's.

The Sheriff cleared his throat, his tone shifting slightly. "Actually, there's something strange I wanted to mention. Heard from Matilda this morning. She found a package on her doorstep, wrapped up all nice and neat, but with a note that just said, 'On the first night.' Gave her a bit of a scare, but she's convinced it's just a prank."

Jason frowned, rubbing his chin. "You think it's a joke, or something you oughta look into?"

Emmett shrugged. "Hard to say. Just thought I'd keep an ear out, in case more of these packages show up. Don't want folks feeling uneasy, especially this time of year."

Micky leaned in, eyes narrowing thoughtfully. "Could be harmless... or it could be someone trying to stir up trouble. Either way, it's curious, wouldn't you say?"

Taylor, who'd been listening quietly, glanced around the table. "If you hear of anyone else getting one of these... gifts, I'd like to know. Feels like there's been enough unease in this town already."

Everyone murmured in agreement, and the topic shifted back to lighter things, but an undercurrent of unease lingered. Matilda's odd gift had left them with a sense of something lurking, just on the edges of their cheerful holiday season. It was hard to shake the feeling that this Christmas might bring more than just good tidings.

As the morning wore on, people gradually left *Bayou Bliss*, heading back to their routines. Cindy stopped by *Burning Love* to open for the day, Loretta had to run some errands, and Jason returned to the bar, ready to prepare for the holiday crowd. Taylor headed to her shop, arranging her ornaments with care, while Micky wandered back to his store, deep in thought.

That evening, as the sun set over Bayou Vista, the town settled into a peaceful lull. Christmas lights sparkled along Main Street, casting a warm glow over the sidewalks, and the air was filled with the scent of gumbo and spiced cider wafting from *Tanya's Crawfish*. Inside, the place was lively with locals, holiday music playing softly in the background.

Cindy and her husband, Dondi, had snagged a booth near the back, each of them savoring a steaming bowl of gumbo. Tanya herself had just walked by to greet them, chatting up a storm as always. Cindy leaned back, glancing around the cozy restaurant.

"You know, Dondi," she began, "feels like it's gonna be a quiet Christmas. Almost... too quiet."

Dondi chuckled, taking a sip of his beer. "Quiet's good, hon. After everything we've seen this year, I'll take quiet."

Just then, the door swung open, and Hank Mullins walked in, his heavy jacket damp from the misty air outside. He spotted Cindy and Dondi, nodding a quick hello as he made his way over. Hank was a regular at Tanya's, always up for a bowl of gumbo and a cold beer.

"Evenin', Cindy, Dondi," Hank greeted, pulling up a chair at their booth. His usual steady gaze was tinged with something unusual tonight, a look that made them pause.

"Hank, darlin'," Cindy said, scooting over to make room, "you look like you've seen a ghost."

He let out a low chuckle, but it was tinged with unease. "Might as well have," he muttered, lowering his voice. "Don't know what's goin' on, but I seen somethin' strange. Real strange."

Cindy exchanged a curious glance with Dondi. "Strange how?" she asked, leaning in closer.

"Well," Hank began, glancing around as if to make sure no one was listening, "for the past two nights, I've been down near the edge of town, checkin' traps by the marsh. Both nights, same time, there's this... figure. Just standin' there. Tall, wearin' a cloak, as still as a statue."

Dondi raised an eyebrow. "You mean a person just standing there?"

Hank nodded. "Don't know if it's a person or not. All I know is, they weren't movin'. Just watchin'... or waitin'. And when I tried to get a closer look, they were gone before I could even blink."

Cindy shivered, rubbing her arms. "Well, Lord, Hank, did you tell the sheriff?"

"I did, yesterday mornin' over at Bayou Bliss. He said he'd look into it, but I think he thinks I'm just gettin' jumpy." Hank sighed, shaking his head. "But I know what I saw. Ain't never seen nothin' like it in all my years fishin' these waters."

Dondi leaned forward, his expression serious. "Maybe it's just someone passing through, someone camping nearby."

Hank shrugged, looking down at his hands. "Could be. Or maybe it's somethin' else. Feels like we're bein' watched, y'know? And after that little package Matilda found on her doorstep... just doesn't sit right with me."

Cindy placed a comforting hand on his arm. "Well, you're among friends here, Hank. We heard about Matilda's package too, so it's clear something strange is going on. We'll keep an eye out, and if you see that figure again, you let us know. We'll make sure the Sheriff takes it seriously."

Hank nodded, visibly relieved. "Thanks, Cindy. Appreciate that."

As they settled back into their meals, the conversation drifted back to holiday plans and family gatherings, but a trace of unease lingered among them. The warm glow of *Tanya's Crawfish* felt a bit dimmer, the festive cheer tinged with an undercurrent of mystery.

By the time they left, the mist had crept in thicker, wrapping Bayou Vista in a quiet shroud.

~ 3 ~

ON THE SECOND NIGHT...

December 14th brought a crisp morning to Bayou Vista, with the town bustling in its usual, cheerful way. Christmas lights blinked from every shop window, wreaths hung on each lamppost, and the air was filled with the scent of fresh coffee and pastries drifting out of *Bayou Bliss*. Lena White, the librarian, pulled her coat tight around her as she walked up the steps to the library, shivering a bit in the cold. She was thinking about the day ahead, about her plans to finish cataloging the holiday book display, when something caught her eye.

There, on the front steps of the library, was a small, odd package. It was wrapped in brown paper, just like the one Matilda had found, and tied with a rough bit of twine. Lena frowned, her heart skipping a beat. She'd heard about Matilda's mysterious gift and the note, and seeing this package gave her an uneasy feeling.

Lena bent down, picking it up cautiously. She held her breath as she read the note attached: "On the second night..."

She sighed, shaking her head. "What in the world?" she muttered, looking around the empty street. Nothing but the quiet town, decorated for the holidays, met her gaze. Curiosity got the better of her, and she opened the package right there on the steps, feeling a chill run through her as the brown paper fell away to reveal a small, broken doll. Its face was cracked, and one arm hung loosely by a thread.

With a puzzled frown, Lena examined the doll. "Well, this is just plain strange," she murmured. Thinking it might be from some local kid playing a prank or maybe something one of the townsfolk left by accident, she decided to head down to *Taylor's Treasure*.

Taylor's Treasure was just around the corner from the library, tucked between *Bayou Bliss* and *Frog's Delight Bakery*. The shop was cozy, filled with antique trinkets, ornaments, and a handful of oddities that made it a local favorite. Taylor herself was inside, arranging a display of ornaments near the window, dressed in her usual sweater and jeans, with a welcoming smile for anyone who walked in.

Lena stepped in, holding the doll carefully in her hands. "Morning, Taylor," she called, her voice a bit shaky.

Taylor looked up, a bit surprised to see Lena so early. "Morning, Lena! You alright? You look a bit pale."

Lena gave a nervous laugh and held out the doll. "I found this on the library steps this morning, all wrapped up like some kind of present. I thought you might recognize it or know if anyone's been buying dolls from here recently."

Taylor furrowed her brow, taking the doll gently. She studied it for a moment, turning it over in her hands. "Huh. Well, I do have a collection of antique dolls in the back, but none of them are broken. And I haven't sold one in... well, a couple of weeks, I think." She glanced up at Lena. "You're sure this was left for you?"

Lena shrugged, rubbing her arms as though she couldn't shake the chill. "I don't know, Taylor. I'm just not sure what to make of it. It feels... strange, y'know?"

Taylor nodded, looking thoughtfully at the broken doll. "Maybe you should take it over to the Sheriff's office, just in case. With all this talk about Matilda's package, I don't know... it's probably nothing, but better safe than sorry, right?"

Lena nodded, grateful for the advice. "You're right, Taylor. I'll head over there now."

The Sheriff, as usual, was at *Bayou Bliss*, enjoying his morning coffee. He sat at a corner table with the Mayor and Micky Vermooch, who had come in for his own cup of coffee, wrapped in his signature wool scarf and knitted cap. The café was filled with laughter and chatter as folks greeted one another, exchanging holiday cheer.

Gail, Patricia, Shannon, and Loretta sat nearby, catching up over lattes and pastries, their voices blending into the pleasant hum of the morning crowd.

When Lena walked in, the small bell over the door jingled, and everyone looked up with curious glances.

She made her way over to the Sheriff, clutching the doll tightly.

"Well, morning, Lena," Sheriff Emmett greeted her, noticing the look on her face. "You alright?"

Lena took a deep breath, her fingers tightening around the doll as she held it out to him. "I... found this on the library steps this morning. It was wrapped up like a present, with a note that said, 'On the second night.' I thought maybe you'd want to see it. Taylor said she hadn't sold any dolls like this recently."

The Sheriff frowned, taking the doll from her and examining it closely. "Looks like Matilda wasn't the only one getting mysterious gifts." He looked at the doll's broken face and arm, shaking his head. "And you say it was just sitting there?"

Lena nodded, her face pale. "Yes. I don't know what to think. First Matilda, and now me... is this some kind of prank?"

The Mayor leaned in, his brow furrowed with concern. "Emmett, you reckon someone's trying to stir up trouble? The timing is... well, it's odd, don't you think?"

Micky, who had been listening quietly, spoke up with his English accent, adding a touch of gravitas to the conversation. "Seems like more than a prank, doesn't it? These aren't the sorts of gifts one leaves just for fun." He gave Lena a gentle, reassuring smile. "Don't worry, love. I'm sure Sheriff Emmett here will sort it out."

Gail leaned over from the next table, her eyes widening as she took in the doll. "Lord have mercy, Lena. That looks like something out of a horror story!"

Shannon nodded, giving Lena a sympathetic smile. "Maybe it's just some teenager trying to scare folks, with it being the holidays and all. But still, it gives me the chills."

Patricia looked thoughtful. "Well, whoever's behind this seems to have some idea about these... 'nights.' Matilda had the first, and now you got the second. Could be someone's idea of a twisted holiday countdown."

The Sheriff set the doll down on the table, rubbing his chin thoughtfully. "Could be. Or maybe it's something more personal. Lena, do you know anyone who'd have a reason to mess with you?"

Lena shook her head, looking around at the friendly faces in the café. "No, not a soul. I just mind my business at the library. Never had any trouble."

The Mayor looked at Emmett, his expression serious. "Well, we can't have folks feeling uneasy right before Christmas. Sheriff, maybe you ought to set up a watch, or at least keep an eye on things around town. Last thing we need is folks feeling unsafe."

Emmett nodded, glancing around the room at the concerned faces of his friends and neighbors. "I'll make sure we keep watch, alright? No need to worry, folks. I'll check in with everyone later, and if anyone sees anything suspicious, you come to me right away."

Micky gave Lena a reassuring nod, his tone gentle. "And you'll be alright, Lena. Whoever left that gift, they're the ones who ought to be worried. This town doesn't take kindly to trouble."

Lena managed a small smile, feeling a bit of comfort in the support of her friends and neighbors. "Thanks, everyone. I just hope it's nothing."

As the day wore on, word of Lena's gift spread quietly through Bayou Vista. Folks murmured about it at the bakery, at *Taylor's Treasure*, and even at *Jason's Bar,* where townsfolk gathered to chat about the strange happenings in town. There was an unease beneath the usual holiday cheer, a feeling that maybe this Christmas wouldn't be quite like the others.

Later that afternoon, Lena returned to the library, but her mind was far from the usual tasks. She found herself glancing out the window, half-expecting to see someone standing out there, watching. The doll and the note had unsettled her more than she cared to admit, and she couldn't shake the feeling that someone was out there, waiting for the next move.

Back at *Bayou Bliss*, the Sheriff and Micky lingered long after the morning rush had died down, discussing the situation in hushed tones. The Mayor had left to attend to some town matters, but Emmett and Micky stayed, talking over their coffees.

"You think it's a prank, or do you reckon there's something more to it?" the Sheriff asked, looking at Micky thoughtfully.

Micky tilted his head, his eyes thoughtful. "Could be either, Sheriff. But there's a certain... intent, I'd say. Someone's trying to send a message, but what that message is, I haven't the foggiest. The only thing I know is, folks are starting to feel uneasy."

Emmett nodded, his face serious. "Well, if it's just a prank, it's a damn good one. But if it's something more, then we best be ready for whatever comes next."

Micky raised his coffee in a quiet toast, his expression grim. "Here's to hoping it's nothing more than some twisted holiday cheer."

They both sipped their coffee in silence, each of them lost in thought, wondering just what kind of mystery had settled over their small town.

~ 4 ~

THE WATCHER'S PRESENCE

The night had settled over Bayou Vista like a thick, quiet blanket, muffling the usual hum of activity. This was no ordinary night, though. For the first time in thirty years, snow had begun to fall, just a light dusting that swirled in the crisp air and caught in the glow of the Christmas lights. It was thin, barely sticking, and would likely vanish by morning, but the sight of snowflakes drifting down on Bayou Vista added a touch of magic—and mystery—that was almost surreal. Folks gazed out their windows, murmuring in amazement, some of the older townsfolk saying they couldn't remember the last time they'd seen anything quite like it.

Inside *Jason's Bar*, the warmth and laughter of the holidays felt comforting against the strange tension. Dondi, Cindy, Shannon, Taylor, Loretta, Tricia, and Jill had gathered at a corner table, whispering about the day's bizarre events. Jason had outdone himself with decorations this year—garlands of pine hung above the bar, red ribbons were tied to the stools, and a small tree, trimmed with red and gold, twinkled softly by the window. But even the holiday spirit couldn't fully chase away the strange feeling in the room.

"Alright, Shannon," Cindy Morrow said, leaning forward with a concerned look. "Tell us what happened this morning at the library. I heard Lena found something strange, but folks are being all secretive about it."

Shannon lowered her voice, glancing around as if someone might overhear. "Well, y'all know about Matilda's package, right? That one left on her doorstep with a note saying, 'On the first night'?"

Loretta nodded, crossing her arms. "Yeah, but I thought that was some kinda prank."

"That's what we all thought," Shannon replied, her voice tense. "But this morning, Lena found a little package just like it on the library steps. Wrapped in brown paper, tied with twine, and with a note that said, 'On the second night.'"

Tricia shook her head, muttering, "Lord help us. What was in it?"

Shannon took a shaky breath. "It was a doll—one of those old, porcelain types. Only this one was broken. Its face was cracked, and one arm was just barely hanging on by a thread."

Tricia shuddered, hugging her coat tighter. "That's... creepy. You reckon it's some kid trying to scare folks?"

"Maybe," Dondi said, but his voice wasn't very convincing. "But who goes around leaving old, broken dolls as pranks? And that note... 'On the second night'? Sounds like someone's got a plan."

Just then, the bell over the bar's door jingled, and Micky Vermooch stepped in, pulling his scarf tight against the cold as he gave the room his usual friendly nod. The Englishman, with his charming accent and quiet presence, had a way of easing people's worries, and tonight was no different. He spotted the group and made his way over, taking a seat next to Taylor.

"Evening, everyone," he greeted, giving a warm smile. "Mind if I join you lot? Heard there's some strange business about."

Loretta gave him a grateful smile. "Micky, you're just in time. Seems we've got a bit of a mystery on our hands."

Micky raised an eyebrow, intrigued. "A mystery, you say? Well, color me curious."

Shannon filled him in, recounting the story of the packages and the figure people had seen standing around town, watching. Micky listened closely, his face growing more serious as she spoke.

"So, folks have seen someone in dark clothing, just standing around, watching?" he asked, his English accent adding a touch of gravity to the words.

Taylor nodded. "Yep, and it's been getting closer, Micky. First, folks thought it was just something out by the marsh. But tonight, it was spotted by *St. Theresa's Church*, then outside *C&D Kwik Stop*, and even across from here, at *Jason's Bar*."

Micky leaned back, looking thoughtful. "Does sound unusual, doesn't it? You'd think whoever it is would have better things to do than lurk around town, scaring folks. But I'll say this—it doesn't sound like any prank to me."

Cindy leaned forward, her face serious. "So, what do we do? We can't just sit around waiting for this... this Watcher to pop up again. People are on edge, Micky. Lena was downright spooked, and it's making everyone nervous."

Micky's mind raced, an unsettling thought taking hold. *If it's Micah—or whoever the killer is lurking out in Devil's Marsh—then this town is in for more than just a fright.*

Before Micky could respond, Sheriff Emmett stepped in, dusting off his hat as he made his way over to the table. He gave everyone a nod and pulled up a chair, resting his hands on his knees.

"Well, I see everyone's got their noses to the ground tonight," he said with a chuckle, though his eyes were serious. "I've been hearing all about this Watcher business, and I can tell y'all, I don't like it one bit. The last thing this town needs is people feeling uneasy, especially this close to Christmas."

Tricia sighed, rubbing her arms as if trying to shake off a chill. "Sheriff, it's just... it's hard to feel safe with someone creeping around town, leaving strange gifts. And those notes—'On the first night,' 'On the second night'—it feels like it's building up to something."

The Sheriff nodded, glancing at Micky. "Well, I reckon if anyone's got a good eye for strange happenings, it'd be you, Micky. Any thoughts?"

Micky tapped his fingers on the table, his gaze distant as he considered the question. "Sometimes, Sheriff, these things are like shadows—they linger, unsettle us, but often reveal nothing more than the fears we carry with us. That said, I wouldn't dismiss it out of hand." He leaned forward, looking each of them in the eye. "Someone may be trying to send a message. What that message is, well, we don't know yet."

Shannon leaned closer. "So you think there's more to it, Micky? This isn't just some prank?"

Micky hesitated, choosing his words carefully. "It's possible someone's trying to get our attention. But let's not let fear take over, eh? Bayou Vista's a good town with good people. We'll get through this."

The Sheriff nodded. "I'll make sure we've got extra patrols around town, just to be safe. But y'all keep your eyes and ears open, too. If anyone sees something strange, come straight to me. We'll get to the bottom of this, together."

The group murmured their agreement, a little comforted by the Sheriff's assurance. For a moment, they fell into silence, listening to the faint strains of Christmas music playing from the jukebox. Outside, the lights on Main Street sparkled, and the snow continued to fall softly, coating the town in a thin layer of white that almost made the strange happenings feel like a dream.

Jill, who had been quiet for most of the conversation, spoke up. "I know this might sound silly, but... doesn't it feel like there's something different about Christmas this year? Like there's a shadow hanging over it."

Taylor patted her hand. "It's not silly, Jill. I think we're all feeling it. But maybe that's why we need to stick together, stay close. The holidays are about family, about taking care of one another. We'll get through this, strange happenings and all."

Micky lifted his mug of coffee, giving them all a reassuring smile. "To Bayou Vista—and to keeping our spirits up, no matter what mysterious visitors we may have. Christmas is a time for joy, and I'd say we're all due for a bit of that."

The others raised their glasses, joining in the toast. The warmth of *Jason's Bar* seemed to press back against the cold, the laughter and clinking glasses filling the room with a comforting, familiar sound. They shared stories of Christmases past, of holiday mishaps and treasured traditions, and for a while, the worries slipped away.

When the evening drew to a close, they bundled up and stepped out into the cold night. The streets of Bayou Vista were quiet, the snow blanketing everything in a peaceful hush. The Christmas lights twinkled softly, casting warm colors over the snow, and for a moment, it felt like any other holiday season.

But as they parted ways and made their way home, each of them couldn't help but glance over their shoulder, just once, to make sure they weren't being watched.

Across town, by St. Theresa's Church, a figure in dark clothing stood at the edge of the parking lot, watching silently. It lingered for a moment, then vanished into the night, leaving behind only the faintest trace of footprints in the snow.

And as Bayou Vista slept, the townsfolk couldn't shake the feeling that something—or someone—was drawing closer, watching, waiting for Christmas to arrive.

~ 5 ~

ON THE THIRD NIGHT...

On the evening of December 16th, a thick fog lingered over Bayou Vista, softening the lights and casting the town in a gentle, surreal glow. The holiday decorations and Christmas lights peeked through the mist, twinkling in quiet contrast to the tension in the air. Folks moved about town, talking in hushed voices, glancing over their shoulders, and wondering what the Watcher would bring next.

At *Bayou Bliss*, the heart of the town, warmth filled every corner. Brenda had outdone herself decorating the place for Christmas. Green garlands lined the windows, ornaments hung from the ceiling, and twinkling lights danced along the shelves, giving the shop a cozy, festive feel. The comforting scent of cinnamon rolls and strong coffee wrapped around everyone who entered, but tonight, it couldn't fully settle the unease spreading through Bayou Vista.

Sheriff Emmett, the Judge, and Preacher John sat in their usual spot in the corner, talking in quiet tones over their coffee. A few tables away, Loretta, Tricia, Tanya, Taylor, and Cindy Blevins huddled together, casting glances toward the men. Even Micky Vermooch had made his way to Bayou Bliss, wrapped in his heavy coat and scarf. He nodded at Brenda, ordered his usual black coffee, and took a seat nearby.

The townsfolk had been talking about the strange packages left for Lena and Matilda. Now, a pattern was forming, and people were starting to whisper about "the Watcher." No one knew who the mysterious gift-giver was, but the name had caught on, and folks were on edge. The usual holiday cheer had a different air to it this year.

The bell over the door jingled, and the Mayor walked in, his face flushed from the cold and looking heavier than usual. He gave a nod to the Sheriff and the others, his gaze drifting to the group of women nearby before he finally pulled up a chair at the Sheriff's table.

"Evening, Mayor," Sheriff Emmett greeted him, tipping his hat.

The Mayor settled into the chair with a sigh. "Evening, everyone. Seems we're in for another strange night, aren't we?"

The Judge leaned in, his expression serious. "Strange is putting it lightly. Folks are uneasy, Mayor. Do you reckon this Watcher business has any real teeth to it?"

The Mayor shrugged, glancing around the café. "Hard to say, Judge. But these gifts are real, and that's enough to stir folks up. I don't blame them one bit."

Preacher John nodded, wrapping his hands around his mug. "It's never sat well with me, this kind of talk. Especially not with Christmas right around the corner. This should be a time for peace, not... well, whatever this is."

Cindy leaned closer to her friends, casting a look toward the Mayor's table. "You think he'll say something? Calm folks down a bit?"

Loretta shrugged. "I don't know, but he should. Lena and Matilda getting those packages... everyone's on edge now, wondering who's next."

Tricia nodded, her face a bit pale. "I hope it's just talk, but it feels... different. Like something's coming."

The bell over the door jingled again, and everyone looked up to see a young boy walk in, barely thirteen, holding a brown paper package. His wide eyes scanned the room, and he spotted the Mayor, walking over to him with a hesitant step.

"Uh, Mr. Mayor, sir?" the boy said, his voice trembling.

The Mayor looked up, frowning. "What is it, son?"

"This... this was left for you," the boy said, extending the package. It was wrapped in the same plain brown paper as the previous ones, tied with a bit of rough twine. The entire coffee shop went silent, every eye on the boy as he placed the package carefully on the table in front of the Mayor.

"Did you see who left it?" the Mayor asked, his voice low and uneasy.

The boy shook his head. "No, sir. My mom found it on a chair by the back door of your office. She thought it must be important, so she told me to bring it over to you."

Sheriff Emmett and Micky exchanged a worried glance. Micky leaned forward, his expression serious. "Well, seems like the Watcher's got another message, doesn't it?"

The Mayor's hands hovered over the package, hesitation in his eyes. Finally, he reached down, untied the twine, and carefully peeled back the paper. Inside was a single, withered rose, its petals brittle and darkened with age. He lifted it, holding it up for a moment as the room fell completely silent.

Loretta broke the stillness, her brow furrowed. "A rose... left for the Mayor. What do y'all think it means?"

The Mayor looked down at the rose in his hand, seeming lost in thought, his face drawn with something none of them had seen before. The room watched, each person wondering about the meaning behind the rose.

Sheriff Emmett placed a hand on the Mayor's shoulder. "We all got things in our past, Mayor. Maybe this Watcher just wants to stir up a bit of trouble, but don't let it get to you."

Micky nodded thoughtfully, his English accent carrying through the silence. "Aye, sometimes the past has a way of coming back around, reminding us of things we thought were long gone. But it's up to you what you do with that reminder."

The Mayor looked around at his friends and neighbors, each one watching him with sympathy and understanding. He gave a small nod. "Thank you all. I... well, I reckon I'll have to think on this one."

Brenda, sensing the heavy mood, stepped forward with a warm smile and a fresh pot of coffee. "Now, let's not spend too much time frettin'. We got Christmas right around the corner, and I won't let a little mystery spoil it. Sheriff, Mayor, y'all do what you need to, but the rest of us, let's keep our focus on what matters."

The room collectively exhaled, a bit of tension easing as folks nodded in agreement. Preacher John patted the Mayor on the shoulder. "Brenda's right. We're in God's hands, and there's no use worrying ourselves sick. Let's enjoy the season."

The conversation gradually lightened, shifting to Christmas stories and holiday mishaps. Tricia shared a funny tale about her cat climbing the Christmas tree and knocking it over, and Cindy laughed, recounting how her son had once made her a crooked ornament that, though imperfect, was her favorite decoration to this day.

Micky, sipping his coffee, leaned in close to the Sheriff. "I'll keep an eye out, Sheriff. Something tells me this Watcher business ain't finished yet."

The Sheriff nodded, his face thoughtful. "Appreciate it, Micky. And you're right—this is more than just a prank. But we'll handle it. Just like always."

As the evening wore on, the townsfolk finished their coffee, bundled up, and left the shop one by one, exchanging quiet farewells and promises to keep an eye out for each other.

The Mayor lingered for a moment, holding the withered rose in his hand as he walked slowly through the foggy streets. The rose felt heavier than it looked, and he couldn't shake the unease that clung to him as he walked, his footsteps echoing softly through the night.

From the porch of the coffee shop, Micky watched him disappear into the mist. "Looks like the past is catching up to Bayou Vista. Let's just hope we're ready for whatever comes next."

As the clock struck midnight, a chill settled over the town—a quiet reminder that this Christmas would come with more than just gifts and good cheer.

6

A CHILLING HISTORY

December 17th rolled in cold and damp, the kind of day that made you wish you'd stayed in bed a little longer. Fog hung low over Bayou Vista, blurring the edges of the streets and softening the Christmas lights strung across porches and lampposts. The town was quiet, save for the clatter of mugs and the low hum of conversation coming from *Bayou Bliss*, Brenda's coffee shop. Folks drifted in, rubbing their hands together and stomping the chill off their boots. The smell of strong coffee and fresh cinnamon rolls wrapped around them like a warm blanket.

Inside, *Bayou Bliss* was dressed for the season. A garland of fresh pine with twinkling white lights draped the counter, and a small Christmas tree stood in the corner, decorated with ornaments made by the local kids. A faint crackle of holiday music played over the radio, but it didn't seem to lift the unease lingering in the air.

The chatter was different from the usual holiday cheer. People weren't buzzing about Christmas trees or what Santa might bring their kids. Instead, they were whispering about the strange gift left for the Mayor—a withered rose, dark as the bottom of a coffee pot, tied with a crimson ribbon.

The Mayor sat by the big window, his usual spot. His coffee sat untouched, steam curling up and vanishing into the air. He wasn't much for gossip, but that rose had him rattled. He glanced at the door every time the bell jingled, half expecting another strange package. When the door opened again, he stiffened.

In came Rosie Fontenot, strutting like she owned the place. Rosie was as wiry as a fishing line, her gray hair barely contained under an old red scarf. She carried herself like someone who knew just a little too much about everyone else's business, which was probably true. Rosie was the town historian—self-proclaimed, but no one dared argue. If there was a secret buried in Bayou Vista, Rosie had dug it up and written it down.

"Mornin', Mayor," she called, her voice carrying over the low hum of conversation. Every head in the shop turned her way. Rosie loved making a grand entrance.

"Morning, Rosie," the Mayor replied, his tone wary. "You look like you've got something on your mind."

Rosie grinned and made her way to his table, pulling out a chair like she'd been invited. "Don't I always?"

Brenda came over with a fresh cup of coffee and a smile. "Here you go, Rosie. Try not to scare off my customers too early, alright?"

Rosie chuckled, wrapping her hands around the mug. "Can't make any promises, Brenda. The truth's got a way of rattlin' folks."

The Mayor leaned forward, his elbows on the table. "What truth are we talking about this time?"

Rosie took a sip, drawing out the moment. The room went quiet, everyone leaning just a little closer. She glanced around, making sure she had their full attention.

"You've heard the stories about Preacher's Pond, haven't you?" she began. "The folks who've gone missing on Christmas Eve? It's not just women. Men and children, too. They vanish like smoke, and no one ever finds a trace."

A murmur ran through the room. Loretta, sitting at a nearby table, frowned. "You mean like ghost stories, Rosie? Or real people?"

"Real as you and me, Loretta," Rosie replied. "Take Mary Ellen White. Back in 1948, she was sixteen, red hair like fire, and a smile that could charm the scales off a gator. She disappeared one Christmas Eve, just as a snowstorm rolled in."

"Snowstorm?" Brenda cut in, raising an eyebrow. "Rosie, it hardly ever snows here, and when it does, it's gone quicker than a gumbo pot at a church supper."

Rosie gave her a sly smile. "Don't mean it didn't happen. Folks say she'd had a fight with her mama and went out walkin' by the marsh, on the other side of Preacher's Pond. Others say she was meetin' a boy. Either way, when the storm hit, Mary Ellen was gone. Come morning, there wasn't hide nor hair of her."

Across the room, a man in a worn jacket stood abruptly, his chair scraping against the floor. He muttered something about needing to check on his wife and hurried out, his face pale. The door jingled behind him, leaving an uneasy silence in his wake.

Micky, who'd been sitting quietly at the counter, leaned back in his chair. His English accent cut through the room like a knife. "And no one ever saw her again? Not a shred of evidence?"

Rosie's eyes twinkled. "Not alive, they didn't. But plenty of folks have seen her ghost—just a flash of red hair or a shadow movin' along the pond. Always around Christmas, and always when the snow falls."

"Rosie, we ain't had a heavy snow in thirty years," Loretta said with a laugh, though her face was pale.

"And what do you think that was the other night?" Rosie shot back. "Didn't look much like rain to me."

The Christmas lights flickered, drawing nervous glances. A draft swept through the room, carrying the faint scent of something metallic. Micky tilted his head, his eyes narrowing as if he'd felt something shift.

"In England," Micky began, his voice low and thoughtful, "there's an old tale about the spirits of the lost. They don't just wander aimlessly. They seek something—justice, resolution, or sometimes revenge. Maybe this Watcher's not so different."

Rosie nodded. "Justice, huh? Seems like this town's got plenty to answer for."

Cindy Blevins, sitting at a corner table near the Christmas tree, spoke up. "But why now, Rosie? Why stir all this up after so long? I mean, if this Watcher's been around for years, why start leaving roses now?"

Rosie raised her mug in a mock toast. "Maybe Bayou Vista's got some reckonin' to do. Maybe the Watcher's just here to make sure we don't forget."

The Mayor let out a laugh, throwing up his hands. "Come on, Rosie! How on earth could I be connected to Mary Ellen? For Christ's sake, I wasn't even born back then!"

Rosie tilted her head, her lips curling into a mischievous grin. "Well, chances are you gave someone a rose, and now that person's with Mary Ellen."

The room broke into laughter—everyone except the Sheriff, who remained stone-faced—while some folks shook their heads at the absurdity of it.

Sheriff Emmett, leaning against the counter, cleared his throat. "Rosie, you really think this Watcher's trying to send a message?"

Rosie met his gaze, her voice dropping to a near whisper. "I don't think, Sheriff. I know. Trouble's knockin' at our door, Mayor. I reckon you feel it too, don't you?"

The Mayor rubbed his chin, glancing out the window toward the pond. The fog clung to the edges of town, thick and heavy, like it was hiding something. He sighed and shook his head. "Rosie, you've given us plenty to think about. But I think we don't need to go stirring up trouble where there ain't none."

Micky raised his mug with a wry smile. "To Bayou Vista, then. To ghosts, reckonin's, and Rosie Fontenot, who never fails to keep us entertained."

A few nervous chuckles rippled through the shop, and folks raised their mugs in a half-hearted toast. But the unease lingered. One by one, they drifted out, their eyes drawn toward the pond as if expecting to see a flash of red hair or hear a voice carried on the wind.

The Mayor paused at the edge of the fog, staring into the distance. Rosie watched him from the window, her expression unreadable, her eyes gleaming with something that wasn't quite satisfaction.

"If you're ready to face what's out there, Mayor," she murmured to herself, "you know where to find me. Just be sure you're ready for the truth—it doesn't always sit easy."

The fog swallowed him as he walked toward Preacher's Pond, his figure fading into the gray. Inside, Rosie sipped her coffee, her eyes drifting to the Christmas lights twinkling above the counter. For a moment, they flickered again, and a chill settled over the room.

Somewhere in the distance, the faint sound of bells echoed, carried on the damp December air. Rosie smiled to herself. Christmas was coming, and with it, the truth. Bayou Vista wasn't done with its ghosts just yet.

7

FOLLOWING THE WATCHER

Bayou Vista was buzzing by mid-afternoon. The fog had lifted some, but the chill remained, sinking deep into the bones of the small Louisiana town. Christmas lights blinked from porches and windows, casting cheerful bursts of color against the gray sky. From *Tanya's Crawfish*, the savory aroma of gumbo wafted out, mingling with the faint tang of woodsmoke in the crisp air.

At *Bayou Bliss*, Brenda busied herself wiping down the counter, though her mind wasn't on the task. The talk about Mary Ellen and the Watcher lingered in her thoughts, unsettling her more than she cared to admit. The bell above the door jingled, pulling her from her reverie.

Loretta, Tricia, Gail, and Patricia walked in, bundled up in coats and scarves, their laughter cutting through the quiet hum of the coffee shop.

"Y'all look like you're headed to the North Pole," Brenda teased, setting her rag aside.

"Feels like it," Loretta replied, blowing on her hands. "Tricia had us stop by her house to grab scarves. Said we weren't 'festive enough.'"

Tricia grinned and adjusted her brightly colored scarf. "It's Christmas, y'all! If we're going to be out and about, we might as well look the part."

Brenda chuckled as she poured coffee into mugs and slid them across the counter. "Speaking of Christmas, y'all hear any more about that rose the Mayor got? Folks can't stop jawin' about it."

Patricia sighed, tugging off her gloves. "We were just at Tanya's place, and it's all anybody's talking about. You'd think somebody found pirate treasure buried under the pond."

"Or a ghost," Gail said quietly, stirring sugar into her cup.

The room fell silent, each woman glancing at Gail.

Brenda leaned against the counter, lowering her voice. "You don't think this has something to do with the Watcher, do you?"

Before anyone could respond, the door slammed open, and Tanya bustled in, cheeks pink from the cold and hair windblown. "I knew I'd find y'all here!" she declared, her voice tinged with urgency.

Brenda raised an eyebrow. "What's got you all worked up?"

"Somebody saw the Watcher," Tanya said, her voice dropping to a dramatic whisper.

The women exchanged looks.

"Who?" Loretta asked, sitting up straighter.

"Old Mr. Guidry," Tanya replied, plopping onto a stool. "Said it was standing by the old oak grove, just staring. But when he tried to get closer, it disappeared."

Patricia rolled her eyes. "That man's always seeing things. Didn't he think the delivery driver was robbing the bank last month?"

"Maybe," Tanya admitted, "but this time, he ain't the only one. Miss Darla from the church office saw it too. Said the same thing—it was just there, then gone."

Brenda tapped her fingers on the counter. She didn't believe in ghosts or spirits, but the stories were starting to stack up.

"Well," Loretta said, her tone decisive, "we're not going to figure this out sitting here drinking coffee. Maybe we ought to go take a look."

Brenda froze mid-wipe. "You wanna go chasing after something nobody can explain? Loretta, that's a bad idea."

Loretta shrugged. "Maybe, but I don't like not knowing. You scared, Brenda?"

Brenda glared at her but didn't answer.

"I'm going," Gail said, her tone steady. "I don't like the idea of something strange hanging around my town."

Tricia bounced on her toes. "I'll come too, but if this turns into a horror movie, I'm blaming you, Loretta."

Patricia hesitated but nodded. "Fine. But if I trip and fall, y'all better not leave me."

The group laughed nervously, but Brenda noticed her hands were shaking as she locked the register. She thought about all the times she'd dismissed ghost stories as foolishness. Maybe she was wrong.

An hour later, bundled in coats and armed with flashlights, the women made their way to the old walking trail. The dirt path wound past the church, the trees looming overhead like crooked sentinels.

"This feels more like Halloween than Christmas," Tricia joked, though her voice quivered slightly.

"Creepy as all get-out," Tanya muttered, glancing around.

Brenda tightened her scarf, her breath puffing in the cold air. She couldn't shake the feeling that the temperature had dropped even further. A faint metallic tang lingered in the air, sharp and unpleasant.

"Y'all feel that?" Brenda asked, her voice barely above a whisper. "It's like the air just... stopped."

The group froze, the stillness around them pressing in.

"Y'all hear that?" Patricia whispered, her voice trembling.

Everyone stood motionless, straining to listen. A faint jingling sound floated on the breeze, almost like sleigh bells.

"That's just somebody's decorations," Loretta said, though her tone lacked conviction.

"Out here?" Gail countered. "Who's putting up Christmas lights in the woods?"

No one had an answer.

The group pressed on, their footsteps crunching on the dead leaves and dirt. Suddenly, Tricia grabbed Loretta's arm.

"There," she hissed, pointing ahead.

The women squinted into the distance. Near the edge of the grove, a figure stood motionless, tall and thin, dressed in dark clothing.

"What the hell?" Tanya whispered, gripping Brenda's arm.

Loretta raised a hand, signaling for silence. They crept forward, the crunch of their boots unbearably loud in the stillness.

When they were about twenty feet away, the figure turned its head ever so slightly, as if acknowledging their presence.

"Hello?" Gail called, her voice steady but firm.

The figure didn't respond.

Patricia took a cautious step forward, but the figure dissolved into thin air, vanishing without a sound.

"Did y'all see that?" Tricia asked, her voice trembling.

"I saw it," Loretta said, her wide eyes glued to the spot where the figure had stood.

"Where the hell did it go?" Tanya demanded, spinning in a circle.

"It wasn't there to begin with," Patricia murmured.

Brenda crossed her arms tightly. "This ain't normal. People don't just disappear like that."

Gail walked toward where the figure had been, scanning the ground. "No footprints. No broken branches. Nothing."

Loretta exhaled sharply. "This ain't just some ghost story anymore. Whatever's happening here, it's real. And it's dangerous."

Brenda shivered, the metallic tang in the air sharper now. Her skepticism was crumbling, replaced by a gnawing fear she couldn't shake.

When they finally returned to Bayou Bliss, the coffee shop felt like a haven. Brenda locked the door behind them, her hands still trembling.

The group huddled around a table, mugs of hot coffee warming their chilled fingers.

"We have to tell somebody," Gail said firmly.

"Tell them what?" Patricia countered. "That we saw something that ain't there anymore? People will think we've lost our minds."

Loretta leaned forward. "Maybe not everybody, but we need to tell somebody. Sheriff Emmett or Micky. He knows things about the strange and unusual."

"If anyone could make sense of this, it'd be Micky," Tricia added with a nod. "And honestly, I don't wanna go back out there without him next time."

"Next time?" Brenda's eyes widened. "You think I'm going back after that? Absolutely not."

The women chuckled nervously, though the tension remained. Brenda stared into her coffee, her thoughts swirling. She'd always prided herself on being grounded, logical, but tonight had shaken her to the core.

Outside, the fog crept back in, wrapping Bayou Vista in its cold, quiet embrace. The faint sound of bells jingled again, drifting on the air, a chilling reminder that whatever was out there wasn't finished.

~ 8 ~

ON THE FOURTH NIGHT...

The following day, Bayou Vista came with a heavy frost blanketing the ground, shimmering under the pale December sun. The fog had finally lifted, but the chill in the air lingered, sharper than ever. Christmas decorations blinked cheerfully along Main Street, trying to fight off the unease creeping into the hearts of the townsfolk. At *Bayou Bliss*, the coffee shop was already bustling with its regulars. The warmth of Brenda's cinnamon rolls and fresh coffee provided a temporary escape from the growing tension.

Inside, Cindy and her husband, Dondi, were seated near the window, their heads bent together in quiet conversation. Cindy's bright red coat stood out against the muted colors of the room, and Dondi occasionally nodded, his face unusually serious.

At the counter, Micky Vermooch leaned back on his stool, a steaming cup of coffee in hand. His English accent carried a calm authority as he spoke with Sheriff Emmett. The Sheriff leaned on the counter, his shoulders slumped, looking every bit the worn-out lawman trying to make sense of something that didn't fit into his black-and-white world.

"I tell you, Micky," Emmett said, his voice low, "this thing's got folks jumpy. I've seen fear spread before, but not like this. It's like the whole town's expecting something to go wrong."

Micky sipped his coffee, his gaze distant. "Fear has a way of taking root, Sheriff. And when the soil's fertile, well…" He trailed off, his expression unreadable.

"What soil are we talking about here?" Emmett pressed, frustration creeping into his voice.

Micky tilted his head, his tone calm but edged with something darker. "The kind that's been watered by secrets and buried by guilt. This town seems to have plenty of both."

By the Christmas tree in the corner, Shannon rearranged ornaments. Her humming softened as her glances toward the counter grew more frequent. Across from her, Preacher John nursed his coffee, flipping through his Bible with the air of a man searching for answers he wasn't sure he'd find.

Behind the counter, Brenda kept busy, but her quick movements betrayed her unease. She glanced at the door repeatedly, her mind racing.

The bell above the door jingled, and Melissa Staggs, *the town's schoolteacher*, walked in. Her sharp blue eyes swept the room before she made her way to the counter, pulling off her gloves.

"Morning, Melissa," Brenda greeted, forcing a smile.

"Morning," Melissa replied, rubbing her hands together. "Smells like you've got fresh rolls today."

Brenda poured her a coffee and slid it across the counter. "You heard about the Watcher?"

Melissa nodded, blowing on her coffee to cool it. "Hard not to, with the way folks are talking. But that's not why I'm here."

Sheriff Emmett straightened, his hand hovering over his mug. "Something happened?"

Melissa hesitated, glancing around the room. The weight of the town's gossip hung heavy in the air, and she felt their eyes on her. Cindy was watching with curiosity, Shannon paused mid-ornament, and even Preacher John looked up expectantly. Her fingers trembled as she reached into her bag, pulling out a small silver bell tied with a thin red ribbon. The faint jingle it made sent a chill through the room.

"This was left on my porch this morning," she said, her voice tight. "Along with this." She unfolded a note and laid it beside the bell. The words were written in neat, old-fashioned script: *'A call for help that was never answered.'*

Cindy gasped softly, and Shannon froze, an ornament still clutched in her hand.

Micky leaned forward, studying the note and the bell. "Curious, isn't it?" His voice was calm, but his eyes narrowed. "A message wrapped in a memory. But what sort of memory, I wonder?"

Melissa's face hardened. "I know exactly what it means. And I don't appreciate someone dredging up the past like this."

"What does it mean?" Cindy asked, leaning forward, her hand brushing Dondi's.

Melissa hesitated, the words catching in her throat. She felt the weight of their gazes, some curious, others tinged with judgment. "Years ago," she began slowly, her voice trembling, "one of my students—her name was Emily—came to me after school. She said her dad was hurting her. I didn't know if I believed her, but I told her I'd call someone. I... didn't. I convinced myself it wasn't my place. A month later, she ran away. They never found her."

The room fell silent. Even Shannon, who rarely stopped moving, stood still by the Christmas tree. Preacher John leaned forward, his hands clasped tightly around his mug.

"Melissa," he said gently, "you said you didn't call for help back then, but maybe this note isn't just about you. Maybe it's about all of us. How many times have we looked the other way when we shouldn't have?"

Melissa's eyes narrowed. "So now I'm supposed to feel like this is everyone's guilt? No. This was my failure, and someone's using it to mess with me."

Cindy placed a hand on Dondi's arm, her voice hesitant. "But why now? Why bring this up after all these years?"

Micky tapped the bell gently with his finger, its soft jingle breaking the stillness. "The better question, perhaps, is: why this particular memory? Whoever's behind this isn't just targeting Melissa—they're weaving a narrative. And if I'm right, we're all part of it."

The bell above the door jingled again, and Loretta, Tricia, and Tanya walked in, their faces flushed from the cold. They froze when they saw the group huddled at the counter.

"What'd we miss?" Loretta asked, her eyes narrowing at the sight of the bell.

"Another gift," Brenda said grimly, gesturing toward the counter.

Tricia read the note aloud. "'*A call for help that was never answered.*'" She shivered. "That's... that's heavy."

"Cruel is what it is," Melissa snapped. "Whoever's behind this is playing games with people's lives, and I won't stand for it."

Loretta crossed her arms, her brow furrowed. "Y'all don't think it's the same person behind the Watcher, do you?"

Tanya shook her head. "I don't know, but it sure feels connected."

Sheriff Emmett held up a hand. "Take it easy, everyone. We're going to figure this out. But in the meantime, let's all stay alert."

"And maybe let Micky take a look," Shannon added. "He's got a knack for figuring out the strange and unusual."

Micky smiled faintly. "Happy to help, of course. Though I do wonder what tomorrow will bring."

A faint jingling sound echoed through the room, the same soft chime as the bell, but no one had touched it. Everyone exchanged uneasy glances, their voices dropping to murmurs.

Brenda stepped back to the counter, the weight of the conversation settling over her. She couldn't shake the feeling that something much bigger was at play.

Outside, the frost glistened in the light. And in the distance, the faint sound of bells jingled again, as if reminding Bayou Vista that the past never stays buried for long.

~ 9 ~

SUSPICION & FEAR

Bayou Vista's streets shimmered under the soft glow of Christmas lights, each string twinkling like stars against the backdrop of the cool Louisiana night. The frosty air bit at exposed skin, and boots crunched over frozen patches on the cobblestone streets. The festive decorations should have brought warmth, but the town remained tense. The Watcher was on everyone's lips, and the icy chill that crept into conversations had nothing to do with the weather.

Inside *Bayou Bliss Coffee House*, the usual hum of chatter was quieter, more subdued, though the room wasn't silent. Brenda worked the counter with brisk efficiency, her movements quick but purposeful. The rich scent of cinnamon rolls and freshly brewed coffee filled the space, creating an inviting warmth, even as unease lingered in every corner.

At a table near the window, Cindy and Dondi from *C&D Kwik Stop* sat close together, their voices low.

Cindy wrapped her hands around a steaming mug, her fingers red from the cold. "I'm telling you, Dondi," Cindy whispered, her voice edged with nervous energy. "It's gotta be someone from town. No outsider could know this much about us."

Dondi leaned back, the wooden chair creaking under his weight. "Or maybe it's someone who's been watching for a while, blending in. Could be anyone, really."

Cindy shivered, tugging her scarf tighter around her neck. "That's even worse. Makes you wonder who you can trust."

At the counter, Micky sat with his usual cup of coffee, its steam curling around his fingers. His English accent cut through the murmurs as he addressed Sheriff Emmett, who stood beside him, his hands resting heavily on the counter.

"Tell me, Sheriff," Micky said, his tone casual but his eyes sharp, "have you considered that the Watcher might be less interested in who's guilty and more interested in who's paying attention?"

Emmett frowned, rubbing his chin. "What're you saying, Micky? That this ain't about justice?"

Micky sipped his coffee thoughtfully. "Not justice, no. Control, perhaps. A puppet master pulling strings to see how we all react."

From the corner of the room, Firecracker, the fiery bakery manager of *Berry's Market*, chimed in. "Or maybe it's just someone with a bone to pick. Folks don't go digging into your past unless they've got a reason."

Across the room, Melissa Staggs, *the schoolteacher,* stiffened. Her hands gripped her coffee mug so tightly her knuckles turned white.

"Melissa, you've been awful quiet," Firecracker said, her voice tinged with suspicion. "Don't suppose you've got something you'd like to share?"

Melissa's eyes snapped up. "What's that supposed to mean?"

"It means," Firecracker continued slowly, turning her piercing gaze toward Melissa, "you were one of the first to get tangled up in this mess. Makes a body wonder why."

Melissa's head snapped up, her blue eyes blazing with indignation. "I wasn't the first," she said, her voice trembling with barely contained anger. "I was just the first to figure out what it meant."

Brenda shot Firecracker a warning look as she set down a tray of steaming mugs. "Now, let's not go pointing fingers where they don't belong. Melissa didn't ask for this, same as the rest of us."

"Well, she sure seems to have an opinion on it," Firecracker muttered, earning a sharp glare from Cindy.

Melissa stood abruptly, her chair scraping against the floor. "You think I wanted this? That I enjoy being reminded of the worst mistake I ever made?" Her voice cracked, and the room fell silent.

She gripped the back of her chair, her knuckles white. "It wasn't just Emily's dad who failed her. It was me. I told her I'd call someone. I didn't. I thought it wasn't my place, or maybe I just didn't want to get involved. And now, every time I close my eyes, I see her face. So yeah, I have an opinion."

The bell above the door jingled, breaking the tension, and Loretta Cobb, Tricia, and Jill walked in, their faces red from the cold. They stomped their boots on the mat, shaking off the chill.

"Did we interrupt something?" Loretta asked, her gaze darting around the room, catching the heated expressions.

"Just the usual drama," Brenda said quickly, motioning them toward the counter. "Coffee?"

Tricia sat down with a dramatic sigh. "We could use something stronger, but coffee will do. What's going on now?"

"Firecracker's stirring the pot," Cindy said with a smirk, earning a mock glare from the bakery manager.

"I ain't stirring nothing," Firecracker shot back. "I'm just saying what everyone else is thinking."

"Well, stop thinking so loud," Brenda muttered as she poured three cups.

Outside, preparations for the Christmas tree lighting ceremony were nearly complete. The towering pine stood proudly in the center of the square, its branches heavy with handmade ornaments and wrapped in strands of white lights. The occasional sound of carolers warming up added to the festive air, though it wasn't enough to chase away the whispers of doubt among the gathered townsfolk.

Tina, Stephanie, and Mary from *Bayou Belle Beauty* worked together to string garlands along the gazebo, their gloved hands fumbling with ribbons and bows.

"You think it's someone we know?" Stephanie asked, her voice barely audible over the sound of boots crunching frost nearby.

Tina shrugged, tying a bow onto the railing. "Could be. But if it is, they're awfully clever."

"Or awful cruel," Mary added, glancing nervously toward the growing crowd. "I just hope this tree lighting gives folks something to smile about."

Near the edge of the square, Taylor from *Taylor's Treasures* was setting up a small booth of holiday trinkets. Preacher John strolled over, his long coat flapping slightly in the breeze.

"Taylor," he greeted warmly, his deep voice steady. "How's business?"

"Not bad, Preacher," she replied with a faint smile. "Though it's hard to enjoy when everyone's so on edge."

John nodded, his face somber. "Fear does that. Makes people see enemies where there are none."

Taylor hesitated, her voice soft when she finally spoke. "You think we'll find out who's behind this?"

"I hope so," John said, his gaze drifting back to her. His voice was steady, but his expression wavered, showing a flicker of doubt he rarely revealed. "But until then, we have to hold on to what brings us together, not what tears us apart."

By the time the sun dipped below the horizon, the square was alive with activity. Vendors sold roasted chestnuts and hot cocoa, children played near the booths, and the townsfolk gathered around the gazebo. Preacher John stepped up to the microphone, his presence commanding as the murmurs quieted.

"Good evening, Bayou Vista," he began, his deep voice carrying over the crowd. "Tonight, we light this tree not just as a symbol of Christmas, but as a reminder of the light within us all. We've been through hard times before, and we've come through by leaning on each other. Let's not lose sight of that."

The crowd clapped politely, their breaths visible in the cool night air. With a flick of a switch, the tree's lights flickered to life, casting a golden glow over the square. For a moment, the tension seemed to lift, laughter bubbling up as children clapped and carolers began to sing.

As John stepped away from the microphone, his shoulders slumped slightly. He gazed at the tree, his lips moving in a quiet prayer. *Lord,* he thought, *if we've ever needed Your guidance, it's now.*

Near the edge of the crowd, Micky turned to Emmett, his tone low. "Well, Sheriff," he said, "there you have it. A bit of light goes a long way."

Emmett nodded, though his eyes scanned the square. "Let's hope it's enough to keep folks from tearing each other apart."

As the night wore on and the square emptied, the festive warmth faded, leaving behind the cold bite of winter. The lights on the Christmas tree twinkled against the dark sky, a hopeful beacon in a town struggling to hold itself together.

And in the quiet stillness, the Watcher's presence lingered—a subtle but chilling reminder that no one in Bayou Vista was safe from the truth.

~ 10 ~

THE TOWN MEETING

The morning in Bayou Vista started like any other in December—frost clinging to rooftops, boots crunching on frozen cobblestones, and Christmas lights blinking against the pale Louisiana sun. But the air felt different today, heavier.

The townsfolk filed into *St. Theresa's Church,* the town's gathering spot for moments like this, their breath puffing visibly in the cold air. The bells from the church's steeple tolled softly, mingling with the murmurs of conversation as neighbors exchanged anxious glances.

Inside the church, garlands of evergreen and red ribbons decorated the walls, their festive cheer clashing with the somber mood. People filled the pews quickly, the scent of fresh coffee from *Bayou Bliss Coffee House* mingling with the faint aroma of pine and candle wax. The room buzzed with uneasy energy as jackets were shrugged off and whispers filled the space.

At the front, Mayor Steve stood near the pulpit, his clipboard clutched tightly in his hands. Sheriff Emmett stood next to him, hat in hand, his face lined with tension. Preacher John, calm and steady as ever, held his Bible under one arm, though a slight furrow in his brow betrayed his inner thoughts. He glanced over the congregation, wondering how much longer the town could hold itself together under this pressure. *Lord, give me the strength to guide them through this,* he thought briefly, before shifting his expression back to one of calm reassurance.

Memories of past divisions flickered in John's mind—a particularly bitter dispute about land rights years ago, when neighbors had turned against one another. He had prayed for weeks back then, trying to mend fences, and the scars still lingered in the community. *We can't afford to go down that road again,* he thought.

Micky Vermooch leaned casually against the wall near the front, his dark coat brushing the floor as he sipped coffee from a silver mug. His sharp eyes scanned the crowd, observing every nervous shuffle and exchanged glance. He nodded briefly to Shannon, who had arrived early and sat near the front, her arms crossed as she leaned forward, clearly anxious to hear what would be said.

Micky's mind raced as he analyzed the room. *Fear spreads faster than fire in a small town,* he mused, watching as people whispered, shifted in their seats, and avoided one another's eyes. He noted the tight grip Cindy Blevins had on her scarf, the way Lena's pen moved more rapidly across her journal, and Firecracker's sharp glances.

They're looking for someone to blame. If this isn't handled carefully, they'll tear each other apart.

A faint memory flickered—a village from his childhood in England. He could still hear the angry voices rising like thunder during an argument about stolen livestock. Doors had slammed shut, and windows had been hastily shuttered as neighbors accused one another. He could see the old cobblestone streets littered with broken pottery after the disputes turned to violence. *People don't need much to light the match,* he thought grimly. *The fire will do the rest.*

Further back, the pews filled with familiar faces. Jason Reisenbeck, from *Jason's Bar,* sat near the middle, his gruff appearance softened by the worried look on his face. He drummed his fingers on his thigh, glancing at the pulpit impatiently. Beside him, Lena, *the town's librarian,* scribbled notes in a small journal, her expression focused. Cindy and Dondi, from *C&D Kwik Stop,* sat a few rows behind them, whispering back and forth, their voices too low to catch but their worried expressions clear.

Near the aisle, Tina, Stephanie, and Mary, from *Bayou Belle Beauty,* huddled close, their heads bent together in quiet conversation. Occasionally, one of them would glance up nervously, as though expecting the Watcher to suddenly appear among them.

The back of the room was no less lively. Loretta Cobb, Tricia, and Jill whispered among themselves, their faces serious. Firecracker, from *Berry's Market,* sat stiffly, her arms crossed as she glared at the front, clearly impatient.

Across the aisle, Taylor, from *Taylor's Treasures,* adjusted her scarf, her face pale but resolute.

Mayor Steve stepped up to the microphone, tapping it a few times until the room quieted. He cleared his throat, his voice steady but strained. "Good morning, everyone. Thank you all for coming out. I know these last few nights have been tough on all of us, and we're here today to talk about what we're going to do about it."

The crowd buzzed with murmurs, some nodding in agreement while others exchanged skeptical glances. Steve held up a hand for silence. "We've all seen what's been happening. The Watcher's leaving notes, stirring things up. And we're working hard to figure out who's behind this, but we need your help too."

Sheriff Emmett stepped forward, his voice carrying over the crowd. "We know the messages are personal, and they're digging up things some folks would rather keep buried. That's deliberate—it's meant to divide us. We can't let that happen."

A murmur swept through the pews. Jason leaned forward, his voice gruff but controlled. "What are we supposed to do, Sheriff? Sit around and wait for the next note?"

"I hear you, Jason," Emmett replied, nodding toward him. "And I get it—this is frustrating. But whoever this is, they're clever. They know the town, and they know us."

"That's just it," Lena chimed in, her voice soft but firm. "Whoever this is knows too much. Women are still missing, strange things keep happening in Devil's Marsh, and now this? It means they're close—maybe even one of us."

The room fell silent at her words, a heavy pause as people shifted uncomfortably. A few exchanged suspicious glances. Cindy Blevins adjusted her scarf nervously, while Tina leaned toward Mary, whispering something that caused her to nod grimly.

As the discussions continued, Micky's sharp gaze caught a subtle movement near the back of the room. A faint creak of the church door echoed as a figure slipped out quietly, boots scuffing against the wooden floor. Shannon glanced toward the noise, her brow furrowing slightly, but when she saw no one she recognized, she turned back toward the front. Micky, however, continued to watch, his expression unreadable. *Curious*, he thought, his mind already filing away the detail for later.

"We work together," Preacher John interjected, stepping to the microphone. His deep voice carried a calm authority, but his eyes betrayed a flicker of doubt. *How do I keep them from tearing each other apart? How do I guide them through something I barely understand?* he wondered silently, though his voice didn't falter. "Fear thrives on isolation. It makes us turn on each other, forget who we are. But we've faced tough times before, and we've come through them by leaning on each other. This time won't be any different."

The townsfolk murmured their agreement, though the unease in the room didn't dissipate.

By the time the crowd began to disperse, the frost outside had begun to melt, dripping onto the cobblestones below. The Christmas lights blinked cheerfully in the square, their glow contrasting sharply with the weight of the morning's discussion.

On the steps of the church, Micky and Emmett lingered, their breath visible in the crisp air.

"You think we made any progress?" Emmett asked, his voice low.

Micky tilted his head, his gaze distant. "Progress? No. But we've stirred the pot, Sheriff. And sometimes, that's all you need to start getting answers."

As the last of the townsfolk trickled out, a heavy silence settled over the square. The Watcher's presence loomed larger than ever. Unseen and unheard, it felt as though they were already planning their next move—or perhaps, had been in the room all along.

~ 11 ~

ON THE FIFTH NIGHT...

The bells on the door of *Bayou Bliss Coffee House* jingled as Shannon stepped inside, holding the sand timer in her hands like it might explode. The warmth of the shop, with its cinnamon and vanilla scents, wrapped around her like a blanket, but the unease curling in her stomach wouldn't let her relax. The golden sands in the timer shifted slightly with each step, each grain falling like a whisper of something terrible just out of reach.

Brenda, standing behind the counter with her sleeves rolled up, raised an eyebrow when she caught sight of Shannon's expression. "Shannon, you look like a hen that's just seen a fox. What's got you so riled up this morning?"

Shannon didn't answer right away. Her boots scuffed softly against the floor as she walked to the counter and set the sand timer down with a soft clink. The room went quiet, the usual hum of chatter and clinking mugs disappearing as everyone leaned in closer to see what she was holding.

Brenda frowned and wiped her hands on her apron. "What is that?"

"A sand timer," Shannon said, her voice barely above a whisper. "I found it sitting on the steps of my shop this morning. Look here." She pointed to the carved letters on the base. "M.E.W."

Sheriff Emmett, seated at his usual corner table with a plate of Brenda's famous beignets, set down his fork and leaned forward. "M.E.W.? You sure about that?"

Shannon nodded, her blonde wavy hair bouncing. "Clear as day, Emmett. You know what it means?"

Before he could answer, the door swung open with a gust of cold air, and Rosie Fontenot strode in, her coat flaring dramatically. "Well, don't everybody hush up all at once!" she exclaimed, grinning like she was about to deliver the best punchline they'd ever heard. "What's goin' on now?"

Without waiting for an answer, Rosie marched straight to the counter. She plucked the timer from Shannon's hands and turned it over with the flair of a magician revealing a trick. Her eyes narrowed as she studied the sands and the intricate carvings. When her gaze landed on the initials, she let out a sharp laugh and slammed the timer onto the counter, making everyone jump.

"Well, ain't this somethin'? *M.E.W.* That's Mary Ellen White," she declared, her voice loud enough to fill the room.

Brenda frowned, crossing her arms. "Mary Ellen White?"

Rosie shot her a look like she couldn't believe the question. "Mary Ellen White. The girl that went missin' back in 1948. You know, the one with the flaming red hair. Pretty as a picture. Disappeared out by Preacher's Pond, near the church."

The room erupted into hushed murmurs. Shannon rubbed her arms, trying to shake the sudden chill that seemed to seep into her bones. "I've lived here my whole life, Rosie. How come I never heard about her?"

"Probably 'cause the old folks didn't want to scare the kids," Rosie said with a smirk. She leaned in conspiratorially toward Brenda. "But I remember my granny talkin' about it. Said Mary Ellen went missin' on a snowy night. And you know what that means."

"There you go with the snow again," Brenda snorted, clearly unimpressed. "Now, Rosie, you're just trying to scare us."

Rosie leaned closer, her voice dropping to a dramatic whisper. "Laugh all you want, Brenda. But you mark my words—if it snows again, that's Mary Ellen. And you know what else?" She paused for effect, her grin fading into something sharper. "The Watcher only comes when it snows. Y'all better start payin' attention 'cause when them flakes start fallin', someone's in trouble."

"Rosie," Emmett interrupted, his voice sharp, "you're not helping. Folks are already spooked enough without you adding fuel to the fire."

Rosie ignored him, gesturing grandly toward the timer. "I'm just tellin' it like it is. This thing right here?" She tapped the base with a loud *thunk*. "It's a message. And it ain't a friendly one."

A shiver ran down Shannon's spine. Her fingers twitched toward the timer as if to take it back, but she hesitated. "But why leave it at my shop? What's it got to do with me?"

"Maybe it's not about your shop, darlin'," Rosie said, crossing her arms. "Maybe it's about you. Or maybe it's just the Watcher playin' games."

Brenda tried to cut through the tension with a forced laugh. "Or maybe it's just some kid trying to pull a prank. Y'all ever think of that?"

"Highly unlikely," Micky said, his rich English accent cutting through the chatter like a knife. He had been sitting quietly near the window with his cup of coffee, observing the scene with the air of someone piecing together a puzzle. Rising gracefully, he strolled to the counter and studied the timer with a thoughtful expression. "The Watcher has been deliberate with every gift left so far, has it not? This sand timer..." He traced a finger along the edge of the base. "It's not just any trinket. Sands nearly gone. Time lost, perhaps? Or time wasted?"

"Or time running out," Shannon murmured, her voice shaking. Her gaze flickered to the frosted window, where the gray sky seemed heavier than usual.

"Exactly," Micky said with a solemn nod. "And if Rosie is correct about Mary Ellen White, this could point us toward something—something we've chosen to forget."

Patricia and Gail from *Pearls & Crystal Cove*, who had just walked in, slid into a booth nearby. Patricia leaned forward, whispering loudly enough for everyone to hear. "My grandpa used to swear he saw her out by the pond the night she vanished. Said her hair was so red it looked like it was on fire."

"That's ridiculous," Brenda said, shaking her head. "A ghost with flaming hair? You've been listening to too many of Rosie's stories."

"Well, maybe not," Gail chimed in. "My momma used to say strange things happened around the pond, especially when it snowed. Do you remember that light snow we had years back? Everything got so quiet afterward, it was like the whole town was holding its breath."

Rosie smirked. "See? Y'all know I ain't just makin' this up. Mary Ellen's tied to Preacher's Pond and the marshland, and the Watcher knows it. That timer's tellin' us time's runnin' out—probably for one of us."

"Enough!" Emmett barked, his tone brooking no argument. He grabbed the timer off the counter and held it up. "I'll hold onto this for now. Shannon, if anything else shows up at your shop, you let me know right away."

Shannon nodded, her voice barely audible. "Fine. But if something bad happens—"

"Nothing's going to happen," Emmett said firmly, though the flicker of doubt in his eyes betrayed him.

As Emmett walked out with the timer, the buzz of gossip in the coffee shop only grew louder. Shannon stayed at the counter, her hands wrapped tightly around her mug of cocoa, her mind racing. She glanced at the window again, watching as a cold breeze scattered a few leaves across the street. A strange, unsettled silence filled her chest.

Rosie's voice cut through the chatter one last time. "Better keep your eyes on that sky, Shannon. Snow in Louisiana's rare, but when it comes..." She grinned, her voice dripping with finality. "It's never for somethin' good."

Shannon shivered and pulled her coat tighter. "Crazy-ass old lady," she mumbled under her breath, but her gaze drifted to the gray sky outside. For the first time, she noticed how the air seemed heavier, colder—like the town itself was holding its breath.

And somewhere deep inside, she felt it too. Something was coming. Something none of them were ready for.

~ 12 ~

ON THE SIXTH NIGHT...

The morning light spilled through the lace curtains in the *Sheriff's Office,* casting a soft glow over the battered desk and the half-decorated Christmas tree in the corner. Sheriff Emmett sat hunched over his lukewarm coffee, his fingers wrapped tightly around the mug. He hadn't slept much, the lines on his face deepened by exhaustion and something heavier—a gnawing feeling he couldn't shake since the sand timer appeared at Shannon's shop.

The knock on the door startled him. "Come on in," he called, his voice rough with fatigue.

Matilda, *the school bus driver,* peeked her head inside, her thick winter coat and scarf bundled tightly around her. "Sheriff, you got something on the porch. Looks like a package."

Emmett's brow furrowed as he stood. "What kinda package?"

"Wrapped in brown paper. I didn't touch it much—just enough to bring it in," she said, handing it over. The twine was wound tightly, and the paper looked worn, as though it had been sitting out for longer than just a few hours.

He took it, the weight in his hands heavier than it should've been. "Appreciate it, Matilda."

"You think it's from the Watcher?" she asked, lowering her voice.

"Most likely," Emmett muttered. "Thanks for bringing it in."

Matilda didn't need any more convincing to leave. The bells jingled softly as the door shut behind her.

Emmett stared at the package for a long moment. His chest tightened as he reached for the pocketknife in his desk drawer. Carefully, he sliced through the twine, letting the paper fall away. His breath hitched when he saw what it was.

An old photograph.

The edges were curled and cracked, the image faded with time. He held it closer to the light, his stomach twisting as he recognized the scene: the town square, decades ago. The gazebo gleamed in the sunlight, its white paint freshly applied. Townsfolk milled about in their Sunday best—children laughing near the fountain, women in flowing dresses, and men tipping their hats with a courteous nod. It was a snapshot of Bayou Vista's past, but Emmett's eyes were drawn to one figure in particular.

In the far corner of the photograph stood a young girl with fiery red hair. Mary Ellen White.

Emmett sat back heavily in his chair, the photograph trembling in his hands. "Damn," he whispered. He could almost hear the whispers of the townsfolk from the stories his mother used to tell, their hushed tones filled with unease.

"That poor girl," she'd said. "She was too pretty for her own good."

The red hair in the photograph burned into his mind like an image from a story he'd heard too many times. He wasn't alive when Mary Ellen disappeared, but he'd grown up in the shadow of her absence. Search parties had combed the marshes, the pond near the church, and every corner of Bayou Vista. They'd found nothing—just rumors, unanswered questions, and a lingering sense of fear that never left the town.

He wondered if the Watcher had chosen him because of his position—or if it was something deeper, something he hadn't realized about himself yet. The thought sent a shiver down his spine.

The door opened, jolting him from his thoughts. Brenda walked in, balancing a tray of steaming coffee cups. "Morning, Sheriff," she said cheerfully, though her smile faltered when she saw his expression. "What's wrong? You look like you've seen a ghost."

"Could say that," Emmett muttered, holding up the photograph.

Brenda's eyes widened as she set the tray down. "Lord have mercy. That's Mary Ellen White, ain't it?"

"Sure looks like it," he replied, his voice tight.

Brenda pulled a chair closer, her gaze locked on the photo. "Where'd you get it?"

"The Watcher left it," Emmett said simply.

Brenda crossed her arms, her face paling. "You reckon it's trying to tell you something? Or just messing with you?"

"Could be either," he said. "But I don't like it, Brenda. This ain't just a coincidence."

The door jingled again, and Micky stepped inside, brushing a faint layer of frost from his coat. "Good morning," he said, his English accent smooth and calm. "I take it the Watcher's been at it again?"

Brenda gestured to the photograph. "Take a look at this, Micky. Tell us what you think."

Micky stepped closer, leaning over the desk to examine the photograph. His sharp eyes scanned the faded image. "The town square... rather charming, isn't it? And this young woman in the corner... Mary Ellen White, I presume?"

"You presume right," Brenda said, her voice barely above a whisper.

Micky leaned back, his expression thoughtful. "And it was left for you, Sheriff? Quite curious. What do you suppose it means?"

"I don't know," Emmett admitted, rubbing his temples. "But I've got a bad feeling about it."

By noon, the story of the photograph had spread like wildfire. At *Bayou Bliss Coffee House*, townsfolk huddled in groups, their voices low but urgent. Rosie Fontenot sat by the window, sipping her coffee with a smirk as she listened to the buzz around her.

"Y'all remember that old rumor, don't ya?" Patricia said, leaning in close to Margie at a corner booth. "About how Mary Ellen was supposed to meet someone at the square that day?"

"Whoever it was, they're probably long gone," Margie replied, stirring sugar into her coffee. "But why leave that picture for the Sheriff?"

"Maybe it's because Emmett's always been curious about the missing women's cases," Brenda chimed in, sliding into the booth with them. "Could be the Watcher knows that."

Rosie chuckled, setting her mug down with a sharp clink. "Oh, Brenda, you think too small. It ain't about Emmett—it's about the town. That picture's a reminder of somethin' we've all tried to forget. And the Watcher knows it."

At the next table, old Mr. Dupree shifted uncomfortably, muttering into his coffee. "The past has a funny way of creepin' back when you least expect it." His words earned a nervous laugh from the others, but the unease in the room was unmistakable.

Across the room, Shannon sat with Micky, her hands trembling as she held her mug of cocoa. "Do you think the Watcher's trying to solve the mystery?" she asked, her voice shaking.

"Perhaps," Micky said, his tone calm but heavy with meaning. "Or perhaps it's simply reminding us of what we've chosen to ignore."

Shannon shivered. "Well, I wish it'd stop. This whole thing's giving me the creeps."

Back at the *Sheriff's Office,* Emmett stared at the photograph again, the weight of it pressing on his chest. The red hair. The laughter in the square frozen in time. The way the town seemed to look the other way when Mary Ellen vanished.

The door creaked open, and Rosie sauntered in, her boots clicking against the floor. "Heard you got yourself a present," she said, her tone teasing.

"Not in the mood, Rosie," Emmett muttered, not looking up.

She ignored him, pulling a chair up to his desk and leaning in close. "You know what I think? I think the Watcher's tryin' to tell you somethin'. And maybe it's time you start listenin'."

"And what do you think it's trying to say?" Emmett asked, his voice laced with irritation.

Rosie leaned closer, her grin fading. "That picture ain't just about Mary Ellen. It's about this town—about what we all let happen back then. Maybe you're supposed to figure out what nobody else could."

Emmett stared at her, his jaw tightening. "And maybe you should keep your theories to yourself."

Rosie laughed, standing and smoothing out her coat. As she reached the door, she turned back, her grin gone.

"You know, Emmett, the Watcher ain't just leavin' gifts for fun. If you don't figure it out soon, someone else might disappear—just like Mary Ellen."

He traced the edges of the photograph again, his mind racing. The Watcher had chosen him for a reason—he just wasn't sure if it was to uncover the truth or to stand witness to whatever came next.

THE HISTORY OF THE GIRL

The bells above the door of *Bayou Bliss Coffee House* jingled softly as Mr. Lueckemeyer shuffled in, leaning heavily on his cane. Known around town as Mr. Lucky, his nickname was as much a nod to his legendary poker games as it was to the countless times he'd somehow dodged trouble in his younger days. The late afternoon light cast long shadows across the polished floors, and the smell of fresh-brewed coffee mingled with the faint scent of cinnamon buns coming from the back. Brenda glanced up from behind the counter, a smile tugging at her lips.

"Well, if it ain't Mr. Lucky," she said, her voice warm and welcoming. "What brings you out this time of day?"

"Needed something stronger than what I've got at home," Mr. Lucky replied, his voice gravelly but laced with a trace of humor. "And maybe a little company."

"Pull up a chair," Brenda said, pouring him a steaming cup of coffee and sliding it across the counter. "You know you're always welcome here."

Mr. Lucky nodded his thanks and eased himself into the chair near the window. Rosie Fontenot was already perched at her usual spot, her legs crossed, a half-empty mug of coffee in her hand. She smirked as he sat down.

"Afternoon, Lucky," she said, raising her mug slightly. "You look like you've got somethin' on your mind."

He let out a long sigh, stirring sugar into his coffee with deliberate slowness. "Don't we all these days? With this Watcher business and that picture of Mary Ellen showing up, it's hard not to think about the past."

Rosie leaned forward, her smirk fading into a more serious expression. "Well, go on, old man. You always were one for stories. What do you remember about Mary Ellen?"

Mr. Lucky hesitated, his fingers drumming lightly against the table. Brenda, sensing the weight of the moment, grabbed her own mug and slid into the chair beside him. The coffee shop had quieted, the few patrons left giving the trio a respectful distance while still straining to overhear.

"It ain't so much about Mary Ellen herself," Mr. Lucky began, his voice low. "It's her family. The Whites. Folks round here don't like talkin' about 'em, and for good reason."

Rosie's eyebrows shot up. "Good reason? I've heard whispers about her daddy bein' mean, but nothin' more than that."

Mr. Lucky shook his head. "Mean don't begin to cover it. Old man White was a tyrant, plain and simple. Ran his house like a ship under siege. The whole family was scared of him—Mary Ellen, her mama, even her little brother, Tommy. That man... he'd do things that'd make your skin crawl."

Brenda winced, her hand tightening around her mug. "Like what?"

"Used to lock Mary Ellen in the closet if she didn't do what he wanted," Mr. Lucky said, his eyes darkening. "Kept her out of school for weeks at a time. Claimed it was 'cause she was sick, but everyone knew better. And her mama? She tried to stand up to him once—once. Came into town with a busted lip the next day."

"Good Lord," Brenda whispered.

Rosie's smirk was long gone now, replaced with a deep frown. "Why didn't anyone do anything?"

Mr. Lucky's laugh was bitter. "You know how it was back then. Folks didn't meddle in what they called 'family business.' Besides, old man White had a way of makin' people look the other way. He was a church deacon, always talkin' about the Lord and morality, but behind closed doors..." He trailed off, shaking his head.

"What about the night she disappeared?" Rosie pressed.

Mr. Lucky's gaze grew distant, as though he were staring back through time. "That night's always been a mystery. Some say she ran off. Others think someone took her. But me? I think she was tryin' to get away from him for good. And I think he knew it."

Brenda's hand flew to her mouth. "You don't think he—"

"I don't know," Mr. Lucky interrupted, his voice heavy. "But I do know this—after she vanished, he stopped comin' to church. The whole family did. It was like they disappeared right along with her."

Rosie leaned back in her chair, her arms crossed. "So, what you're sayin' is the Whites weren't just victims. They had their own mess of sins, and maybe that's what the Watcher's diggin' up now."

"Could be," Mr. Lucky said. "But it ain't just the Whites. This town... we all looked the other way. We let things happen we shouldn't have. That's what keeps me up at night."

The room fell silent for a moment, the weight of his words settling over them like a heavy quilt. Even Brenda, who was usually quick to defuse tension, seemed at a loss for words.

Finally, she spoke, her voice barely above a whisper. "You think that's why the Watcher's here? To make us face what we ignored?"

Mr. Lucky nodded slowly. "Reckon so. And if we don't, I'm afraid this town's gonna tear itself apart."

Micky chose that moment to walk in, his coat dusted with frost and his scarf wrapped tightly around his neck. He glanced around, sensing the gravity of the conversation. "I take it I've missed something significant," he said, his English accent cutting through the quiet.

Rosie filled him in quickly, her words sharp and to the point. When she finished, Micky sat down beside her, his expression thoughtful.

"It's always the way with small towns, isn't it?" he said after a moment. "Secrets buried so deep they become part of the soil. And now, it seems the Watcher's decided it's time to unearth them."

"Yeah, well, I don't much like bein' part of some ghost's revenge plot," Rosie shot back.

Micky chuckled softly. "None of us do, Rosie. But perhaps this isn't about revenge. Perhaps it's about redemption."

"Redemption for who?" Brenda asked.

"For everyone," Micky replied simply.

As the coffee shop buzzed quietly around them, Mr. Lucky stared into his mug, his thoughts clearly miles away. "I just hope," he said softly, "that we're ready for whatever's comin'."

The bells above the door jingled again, and Shannon walked in, her face pale as she clutched a bundle of papers in her hand. "Y'all," she said, her voice trembling. "You need to see this."

Everyone turned to her, the room growing eerily still. Whatever was on those papers, it was clear from Shannon's expression that the Watcher's game was far from over.

~ 14 ~

SNOW IN THE BAYOU!

The bells over the door jingled. Loretta and Taylor burst into the coffee shop, their cheeks flushed from the cold. They stomped the snow off their boots, Their wide eyes darting around the room.

"It's snowing, y'all!" Loretta announced, her voice rising with disbelief. "Not just a little, either—it's coming down like crazy out there!"

Everyone in the room froze. Brenda, leaning over the counter, set her coffee pot down with a clatter. "Snow? Here? Loretta, are you pulling my leg?"

Loretta shook her head, pulling off her hat and shaking snowflakes onto the floor. "Go look for yourself!" she said, motioning toward the window.

Rosie, perched at her usual table, raised an eyebrow before sliding her chair back. "Well, ain't that somethin'," she muttered, making her way to the window. One by one, the rest of the room followed, chairs scraping across the floor as they crowded around the glass.

Outside, heavy snowflakes fell, sticking to the streets, the rooftops, and the branches of the ancient oaks lining the square. The world beyond the coffee shop had transformed into a winter wonderland, but it wasn't magical—it was unsettling.

"It's really snowing," Brenda whispered, her hand pressed against the glass. "Real, honest-to-God snow."

"And heavy, too," Taylor added, her breath fogging the window. "I can't remember the last time I saw it like this."

Mr. Lucky, who had been silently watching, finally spoke, his tone grim. "Thirty years ago. That was the last time Bayou Vista saw snow like this—and it wasn't just the weather that had folks scared."

The coffee shop fell into silence. The snow seemed to dampen not only the sound outside but the mood within. Shannon stood near the counter, holding a bundle of papers tightly against her chest.

"That's what I was trying to tell y'all," Shannon said, breaking the stillness. "These papers—they're about the last snowstorm. About what happened then. About who disappeared."

Brenda turned from the window, her expression unreadable. "Well, don't just stand there, Shannon. Tell us what you found."

Shannon set the papers down on the counter, her hands trembling. "This here," she said, pointing to a yellowed newspaper clipping, "is from that storm. A baby girl, a teenage girl, an old man, and a woman from the

Carr family disappeared—gone without a trace. And the storm? It came out of nowhere, just like this one."

Loretta crossed her arms, her tone sharp. "And you think this storm means someone's gonna disappear again?"

"I don't know," Shannon admitted, flipping through the pages. "But the stories talk about how it felt. The quiet. Like the world had stopped. Folks said they could feel something coming—something bad."

Micky, who had been standing silently by the window, finally spoke, his English accent soft but commanding. "The snow isn't just weather. It's a message."

"A message?" Loretta asked, her brow furrowing.

Micky turned, his expression serious. "When the past is ignored, it doesn't stay buried. It comes back—sometimes with a vengeance. The Watcher isn't just stirring up old memories; it's accelerating them."

Before anyone could respond, the bells above the door jingled again. Emmett stepped inside, his boots caked with snow, his expression grim. He shook off his coat and stomped his feet, sending clumps of snow scattering onto the floor. "We've got tracks out by Preacher's Pond," he said, his voice low. "And they're not human."

The room erupted into murmurs as Emmett moved toward the counter.

"What kinda tracks?" Rosie asked, narrowing her eyes.

"Clawed," Emmett said grimly. "Deep and wide. Like something heavy was moving through there. And they lead straight into the woods."

Shannon clutched her scarf, her knuckles white. "This is starting to feel too much like last time. Snow, disappearances, strange things out by the pond... I don't like it."

Taylor glanced at Emmett, her voice trembling. "Maybe we should go looking. If someone's out there..."

"No one's going anywhere," Emmett interrupted sharply. "Not in this storm. If those tracks are what I think they are, we're dealing with something we don't understand."

"But what if someone's already missing?" Loretta argued, her voice rising. "What if we're too late?"

"We don't know that yet," Emmett replied, his tone steady but firm. "For now, we stay put. No one goes anywhere alone. That's an order."

Shannon sighed, sitting down heavily at the nearest table. "I remember when it snowed last time. I was just a little girl, but I'll never forget the way it felt. My mama kept the radio on all night, listening for news. Told me to stay away from the windows—said the snow brought bad spirits."

Brenda nodded, her voice trembling. "My grandpa used to say the same thing. Said snow wasn't natural here, and when it came, it always meant someone wasn't coming back."

The snow outside thickened, its weight pressing against the windows. The usual sounds of the town—distant voices, a passing car—had vanished, swallowed by the storm's eerie silence.

"Y'all feel that?" Shannon whispered, breaking the stillness.

"Feel what?" Brenda asked.

"The quiet," Shannon replied, her voice trembling. "It's like the whole world's holding its breath."

The wind outside stopped abruptly, leaving only the sound of snowflakes tapping against the glass.

Rosie snorted, though her usual humor was gone. "Let's just hope it exhales before it takes someone else with it."

The coffee shop grew still, the air heavy with anticipation. As the snow thickened, it felt less like a wonder of nature and more like a harbinger of something far darker. And deep down, they all knew the Watcher wasn't done yet.

~ 15 ~

ON THE SEVENTH NIGHT...

The seventh night arrived in Bayou Vista, cloaked in a silence as heavy as the snow falling from the heavens. Outside *Bayou Bliss Coffee House,* Christmas lights blinked softly from the rooftops and lampposts, their colors muted by the relentless snow. A garland wrapped in twinkling fairy lights framed the windows, casting a soft glow inside the café. The air smelled of cinnamon and pralines, and faint strains of "Silent Night" drifted from the old radio near the counter. Yet, for all its holiday warmth, the mood in the room was anything but merry.

Taylor sat at the counter, her hands wrapped tightly around a steaming mug of Brenda's finest dark roast. Her brown curls clung to her face, damp from the snow, and her wide green eyes darted to the door every time the bells jingled. The festive garland hanging above her felt like an insult to the unease clawing at her chest.

"You look like you've been wrung out, sugar," Brenda said, her tone a mix of concern and tenderness. She nudged a plate of pecan pralines closer to Taylor, hoping to coax some warmth into her. "Did Mr. Lucky give you trouble when you walked him home?"

Taylor managed a weak smile, brushing a damp curl from her cheek. "He's as stubborn as a mule, Brenda. Took his sweet time sniffing every lamppost and barking at shadows. By the time we got to his house, I was half-frozen and ready to leave him out in the snow."

Brenda chuckled softly, her hands busy wiping down the counter. "That old dog's got more attitude than sense. But he loves you, you know. He only gives trouble to folks he trusts."

Taylor sighed, wrapping her hands tighter around the warm mug. "Well, he sure knows how to pick the worst nights to act up. It's like he could feel something in the air—kept looking back over his shoulder like he was spooked."

Brenda's movements slowed, her eyes flicking toward the frosted window. "Dogs know things, Taylor. They see what we don't. Maybe it's not just him feeling the storm." She glanced back at Taylor, her voice softer now. "Maybe you're feeling it too."

Taylor didn't answer right away, her gaze fixed on the steam rising from her coffee. "Yeah," she whispered finally. "It doesn't feel right, Brenda. Feels heavy, like it's sitting on my chest."

Brenda nodded as she wiped the counter, her brow furrowed. "You're not the only one feeling it. Everyone's on edge. Ain't natural, this much snow in the bayou."

In the corner, Rosie Fontenot sat cradling her mug of chicory coffee, her eyes scanning the room with a familiar sharpness that even the soft glow of the multicolored Christmas lights around her table couldn't dim. "Last time we had snow like this, bad things happened," she said, her voice cutting through the chatter. "Y'all remember? Folks disappeared, and there weren't no answers."

Brenda glanced up from the counter, her tone laced with exasperation. "Rosie, how many times are you going to remind us of that? We've heard it in every breath you've taken this week."

Before Rosie could fire back, Shannon, perched at a table near the counter, chimed in, her voice thoughtful but grim. A stack of yellowed papers lay in front of her, their edges curling with age. "Brenda, she's not wrong," Shannon said. "I've been digging through the old records all day, and this storm—it's too much like the one thirty years ago. And we all know how that ended."

The room fell silent for a moment, the weight of Shannon's words settling over everyone. Even Brenda, who prided herself on staying calm, seemed to hesitate before she returned to wiping the counter, her movements slower now.

The door jingled as Micky Vermooch strode in, brushing snow off his long coat. His English accent cut through the heavy atmosphere. "Well, isn't this cozy? A bit of snow in Louisiana, and you lot are ready to write your obituaries."

Rosie shot him a glare. "Ain't nothin' funny about this, Micky. This town's been through enough."

Micky smirked, his blue eyes glinting as he loosened his scarf. "Come now, Rosie. Snow doesn't kill people. It's what hides beneath it you ought to worry about."

The room fell into an uneasy silence. Brenda poured Micky a fresh cup of coffee and set it on the counter. "Have a seat, Micky. Don't mind Rosie—she's been on my last nerve all day."

Taylor shifted in her seat, her hands trembling as she reached into her purse. "I found something tonight," she said, her voice shaking.

All eyes turned to her. "What kinda something?" Brenda asked, her concern deepening.

Taylor placed a small, muddy shoe on the counter. It was tiny, barely big enough for a toddler, and worn with age. The faded red fabric was smeared with dirt, and its laces dangled limply. A collective gasp rippled through the room.

Rosie stood abruptly, her chair scraping against the floor. "Lord have mercy," she whispered. "That's a baby's shoe."

Shannon glanced up from her papers, her tone dry. "Well, thanks for pointing that out, Rosie. We never would've figured it out without you."

Taylor's lips quivered as she pulled a folded note from her pocket. Her voice cracked as she read aloud, "'You all know the truth, and so do I.'"

The weight of the words pressed down on everyone, and even the cheerful glow of the Christmas lights seemed dimmer.

Micky's gaze lingered on the shoe for a beat longer than necessary, his expression unreadable. "Whoever left this knew exactly what they were doing," he said, his voice quieter now, almost as if speaking to himself. "Some memories don't stay buried. They just bide their time."

Shannon pushed her papers aside, her voice tight with curiosity and fear. "Where exactly did you find it, Taylor?"

"Right on my porch," Taylor replied, her voice trembling. "Just sitting there like it belonged. The snow hadn't even covered it yet."

Rosie crossed her arms, her voice sharp. "Who'd leave somethin' like that? And why you, Taylor?"

Taylor's voice cracked as tears welled in her eyes. "I don't know. I haven't done nothing to deserve this."

Brenda reached out, her voice soothing as she squeezed Taylor's hand. "Honey, this ain't about you. Whoever's doing this wants us scared. They're digging at something deeper than any of us."

The bells over the door jingled as Sheriff Emmett stepped in, his boots caked with snow and his hat dripping water onto the floor. He took one look at the tiny, muddy shoe on the counter and let out a low whistle.

"Mind filling me in?" he asked, his tone as grim as his expression.

Brenda quickly gave him the rundown, her voice steady but strained. Emmett frowned as he picked up the shoe, turning it over in his hands with the careful precision of someone who'd handled too many tragic artifacts. "This look familiar to anyone?"

Rosie spoke up. "Could be from one of them kids that went missin' thirty years ago. Y'all remember the Carr girl? Clara Mae Carr. She was just a baby when she vanished."

Shannon flipped through her stack of clippings, pulling out a yellowed newspaper article. "She disappeared on the seventh night, too," she said, her voice barely above a whisper. "Just like this storm. No footprints. No signs of a struggle. It was like she just... evaporated."

The room fell silent again, the only sound the soft hum of the radio. Even the faint strains of "Silent Night" seemed to carry a haunting undertone.

Micky leaned forward, his expression uncharacteristically serious. "Whoever left this wanted us to remember. Not just Clara Mae, but what she represents. The question isn't 'why Taylor,' but 'why now?'"

Taylor's fingers trembled as she clutched her mug, her thoughts racing. *Why me? Why my porch?* She stared at the note again, its simple words growing heavier with each glance. Clara Mae Carr's name echoed in her mind—she'd heard it whispered in hushed tones, the mystery of her disappearance a cautionary tale told by worried parents.

But this wasn't a story anymore. It was real. And it was at her door.

"You think it's happening again?" she asked, her voice trembling but strong enough to carry across the room.

Micky's gaze met hers, unflinching. "I think it never stopped," he said softly, the words laced with something darker, deeper.

Emmett stepped forward, the quiet authority of his presence drawing everyone's attention. "Listen up," he said firmly. "No one's going anywhere alone from now on. We check on our neighbors, keep an eye out, and report anything suspicious. We stick together, and we don't take chances."

Brenda nodded, folding her arms tightly across her chest. "Micky's right. Whoever's behind this wants to scare us, but they're not tearing this town apart."

The room murmured in agreement, a faint undercurrent of fear giving way to resolve. Outside, the snow fell heavier, blanketing the streets in eerie silence. But inside Bayou Bliss Coffee House, the warmth of the season and the unyielding strength of a small town stood firm.

~ 16 ~

SEARCHING FOR CLUES

The snow fell harder as the eighth day dawned, smothering Bayou Vista under an icy blanket. The festive decorations on the lampposts and rooftops seemed almost defiant against the oppressive gray sky, their cheerful glow muted by the relentless storm.

Inside the library, however, the warmth of Christmas still lingered. A small tree twinkled in the corner, its lights reflecting off the frosted windows. The air carried the comforting scent of pine, old books, and a faint hint of coffee someone had smuggled in.

Loretta Cobb sat beside Taylor at one of the long wooden tables, flipping through a stack of brittle newspaper clippings. Her face was pale, her long blonde hair tucked beneath a knit cap. The faint hum of the heaters and the rustle of papers filled the room as the two women worked quietly, their determination visible in every movement.

"This doesn't sit right," Loretta muttered, her voice barely above a whisper.

Taylor glanced at her, her own fingers trembling as she turned a page in the records. "What doesn't?"

Loretta hesitated, her brown eyes scanning the headline of an old article. "*Storm of '94: The Carr Family Demands Justice for Missing Daughters.*" Her voice dropped further. "It's like someone wants us to forget what happened. Pages torn out, records missing... It isn't normal."

Across the table, Rosie Fontenot huffed, tapping her nails against a dusty ledger. "That's exactly what I've been sayin'. The Carr family thought this town was coverin' up somethin'. And by the looks of it, they weren't wrong."

Nearby, Cindy Blevins, owner of *Burning Love*, sat hunched over a microfilm reader, squinting at the screen. She wore her signature bright red coat, a stark contrast to the muted tones around her. "Well, I don't know about you," she said, her voice cutting through the room, "but if someone was covering this up, they sure did a sloppy job. Half these records look like they've been chewed up by rats."

Shannon, seated at the same table, looked up from her notes, a hint of a smile softening her tense expression. "That's just how old records are, Cindy. But you're right—some of this damage looks... intentional."

Loretta frowned, pulling another clipping from the pile. "Listen to this," she said, her voice rising slightly. "'*Carr Family Faces Backlash for Accusing Local Officials.*' They were trying to find their daughters, and the town turned against them?"

Cindy shook her head, leaning back in her chair. "People don't like being called out, honey. Especially not in a place like this. Folks here would rather sweep things under the rug than deal with the truth."

Loretta hesitated, running her fingers over the brittle newspaper clipping. "I remember Jill's mom talking about the Carrs. She used to hush up whenever Clara Mae and Emily's name came up, like saying it out loud would bring something bad. One time, I heard her whispering to her sister about how folks in town were acting strange after Clara and her sister Emily vanished—like they knew something they didn't want to say." She looked at Taylor, her eyes filled with unease. "Now I'm wondering if she was right."

As Loretta spoke, the lights overhead flickered briefly, a barely audible hum cutting through the room. Shannon paused, her pen hovering over her notepad. "Y'all feel that?" she murmured.

Taylor nodded, glancing toward the window. The snow outside seemed unnaturally still for a moment, as though the storm itself was listening.

At *Micky's Magical Things,* the shop bustled despite the worsening snowstorm. The golden light from the stained-glass windows spilled onto the icy sidewalk, and the sound of jingling bells announced every new arrival. Inside, the warmth of candles and the faint scent of herbs created a sanctuary from the storm's fury.

Micky Vermooch stood behind the counter, his usual easy smile tempered by the weight of the town's unease.

His rich English accent carried over the hum of conversation as he spoke to a cluster of concerned residents.

"Are we gonna be okay, Micky?" Patricia asked, clutching a tiny crystal angel she'd just purchased. Her voice wavered, her usual confidence replaced by worry.

Micky leaned forward, resting his hands on the counter. "We'll be as okay as we choose to be, Patricia. Fear makes things worse. We stick together, we face it head-on—that's how we get through this."

Jason Reisenbeck, owner of *Jason's Bar*, let out a low grunt from where he stood near the window. "That's all well and good, but what if sticking together ain't enough? What if whatever's out there doesn't care about our courage?"

Micky's gaze shifted to him, calm but firm. "Then we remind it who we are. This town has more fight in it than most give it credit for."

The wind howled outside, rattling the shop's glass door. Snowflakes clung to the edges of the windows, melting into uneven trails. Every time the door opened, a sharp gust of icy air swept in, carrying with it the unmistakable scent of frozen pine.

Back at the library, Sheriff Emmett arrived, snow dusting his hat and shoulders. He greeted Lena, who was tidying the front desk, before making his way to the table where Loretta, Taylor, and Rosie were still poring over records.

"Anything useful?" he asked, his deep voice breaking the silence.

Loretta looked up, her expression grim. "Depends on what you call useful. We know the Carr family was shouting about a cover-up before they left town, but not much else."

Emmett nodded, pulling out a chair. "It's a start. Keep digging."

Cindy arrived a moment later, carrying a large book she'd found in the back of the library. "You might wanna look at this," she said, setting it down with a thud. The leather cover was cracked, and the pages smelled of mildew. "It's a family ledger from around the time Clara Mae and Emily disappeared. Looks like it belonged to the Carrs."

Shannon turned the brittle pages of the ledger, her eyes narrowing as she pointed to a name scrawled in faded ink. "Wait," she murmured, her voice barely above a whisper. "Does this say... Roy Martin?"

Rosie leaned closer, her eyes narrowing as she peered at the ledger. "Loretta's ole step-daddy? What's he doin' in there?"

Loretta froze, her breath catching. She hadn't heard that name in years—not since the night he was found murdered at the old campground. The man who had killed her mother. Her fingers tightened around the edge of the table, the rough wood biting into her palms. "I don't know," she said finally, her voice taut. "But if his name's in here, it ain't for nothing good."

Rosie nodded slowly, her gaze never leaving the page. "That man always gave me the creeps. You reckon he had somethin' to do with Clara Mae and Emily?"

Shannon flipped another page carefully, her brow furrowed. "It's too soon to say, but it feels like we're digging up bones that were meant to stay buried."

The room fell silent, the name hanging in the air like a shadow.

As evening fell, the storm raged on, swallowing the town in a relentless curtain of white. At the *library*, the crackling of brittle pages and hushed murmurs of discovery filled the room. Meanwhile, at *Micky's Magical Things*, the golden light of stained glass reflected on snow-covered streets, a beacon of hope in the storm.

The snow wasn't just weather—it was a presence, watchful and waiting.

As the residents of Bayou Vista pieced together fragments of the past, they couldn't shake the feeling that something—or someone—was piecing together their future. And whatever the truth might be, they were running out of time to uncover it.

~ 17 ~

ON THE EIGHTH NIGHT...

The snow kept falling, a steady curtain of white draping over Bayou Vista like a thick winter quilt. The town had grown quieter as the storm lingered, but life didn't come to a halt—not in a place like this. The heart of Bayou Vista beat strongest in its people, and many of them found themselves gathered inside *Bayou Bliss Coffee House*, seeking warmth and company.

The rich scent of coffee and fresh pastries filled the air, mingling with the low hum of conversation. The place was bustling despite the snow piling outside, a sanctuary of light and heat. Brenda moved swiftly behind the counter, her red-and-black apron a blur as she kept the orders flowing.

"Y'all find a seat, and I'll have something hot out for you in a minute!" Brenda called over her shoulder, balancing a tray of steaming mugs.

Gail, wrapped in a thick gray coat, stomped the snow off her boots as she entered, her cheeks flushed from the cold. "Brenda, this snow just won't let up!"

"You ain't lying, Gail," Brenda replied, setting down a tray on the counter. "I was just saying to Loretta—it feels like this storm has a mind of its own."

Gail leaned in a bit closer, her voice lowering. "I just hope Margie's okay. She had to head to the airport this morning to pick up her brother Eddie. With the roads like this, I've been worried sick."

"Margie?" Brenda asked, her brows furrowing. "She's driving in this mess? Lord have mercy. You tell her to take it slow. Ain't nothing worth rushing in weather like this."

"I did," Gail said, sighing. "But you know Margie. Once her mind's set, ain't no talking her out of it."

Loretta, sitting at a corner table with Taylor and Tricia, waved Gail over. The trio had already staked their claim with mugs of cocoa and coffee, their table cluttered with napkins and an untouched plate of beignets.

Gail smiled and made her way over, unbuttoning her coat as she sat down. "Y'all staying warm?"

"Best we can," Loretta said, taking a sip of her cocoa. "But this weather makes my bones ache, and I ain't even old yet."

"Speak for yourself," Tricia teased. "My bones feel just fine. It's my patience that's wearing thin."

"Mine too," Taylor chimed in, leaning back in her chair with a sigh.

Tricia shook her head, her grin fading into a thoughtful expression. "Ever since these gifts started showing up, things just feel... different."

Before Taylor could respond, the door jingled open, and Micky Vermooch stepped inside, a gust of icy wind following him. He shook the snow off his coat and flashed a smile, his English accent cutting through the warm southern drawls around him.

"Morning, everyone!" Micky greeted, his voice cheerful despite the cold. "I see the snow hasn't kept you all indoors. Brave souls, the lot of you."

"Morning, Micky!" Brenda called, already pouring him a coffee. "Sit yourself down. I'll bring it right over."

Micky nodded his thanks, making his way to Gail's table. "Mind if I join you?"

"Not at all," Gail said, smiling as he pulled out a chair.

The bell over the door jingled again, and Tina swept in. She was carrying a small box wrapped in plain brown paper and tied with twine. Her face was pale, and her usually cheerful demeanor was shadowed by unease.

Brenda called out from the counter, "Tina! You look like you're half frozen, girl. Get over here and warm up."

Tina nodded, making her way straight to the counter. She set the box down gently, almost as if she was afraid to touch it for too long.

"Coffee, Brenda," Tina said, her voice tight. "I need something strong."

"What's going on, hon?" Brenda asked, pouring a fresh cup and sliding it toward her. "What's that?"

Tina nodded, glancing around the room. "It showed up on my doorstep last night. I didn't even hear anybody out there."

The room grew quieter as her words carried across the tables. Micky, seated at Gail's table, leaned forward, his sharp blue eyes fixed on the box. "May I?" he asked, his rich English accent cutting through the hushed murmurs.

Tina hesitated but nodded. "Be my guest. It's why I came here—to take it to the sheriff. Thought maybe someone ought to look at it."

Micky stood and approached the counter, his movements calm but deliberate. He reached for the box and gently untied the twine, his fingers deft as he peeled back the plain paper.

Underneath was a beautifully carved wooden music box, its surface polished to a deep, rich sheen. It was old, the kind of craftsmanship that spoke of another time.

"That's something," Brenda said, leaning closer. "What's it do?"

Micky lifted the lid, and a hauntingly sorrowful tune spilled out, filling the shop. It was a melody that seemed to carry the weight of lost memories and silenced dreams, wrapping itself around everyone in the room.

Tina's hands trembled as she set her coffee down. "That song—it's the same one my granny's music box used to play. She'd wind it up every night before bed when I was little."

Her voice wavered, and she looked down, as if the weight of the memory was almost too much to bear. "She always said it was a way to end the day on a peaceful note. I never thought I'd hear it again, not after she passed. It's like…" Her voice caught. "It's like someone reached into my childhood."

Brenda glanced toward the windows as the song faded. A faint draft seemed to curl through the room, bringing with it a chill that didn't belong in the warmth of the coffee shop. "Did someone leave the door open?"

"No," Gail murmured, her eyes darting around. "But I felt that too."

Micky's expression sharpened. "Places like this remember," he said softly. "And sometimes, those memories find their way back to us."

Tina hesitated before closing the lid. As she did, her voice cracked, and she whispered, "I don't want it. Not in my house, not near me. I'm taking it to Sheriff Emmett—he's got to figure out who's behind this… and why."

"I'll go with you," Loretta offered, stepping closer. "No sense in you going alone."

As Tina and Loretta prepared to leave, Brenda moved to the window, staring out into the swirling snow. For a moment, she thought she saw movement—a shadow flickering at the edge of her vision. She blinked, leaning closer, but the snow fell thick and fast, hiding whatever it was.

Brenda's voice was barely above a whisper as she turned to Micky. "What do you think it means?"

Micky's gaze lingered on the door, his expression unreadable. "Sometimes, objects like this carry more than memories. They carry purpose. And purpose… well, it can be dangerous in the wrong hands."

The coffee shop buzzed with hushed speculation as the morning wore on, but the melody seemed to linger, like a ghost haunting the edges of their thoughts.

Outside, the snow fell harder, blanketing the streets and muffling the world. Somewhere in that silence, unseen eyes waited for their moment to step into the light.

And once again, Bayou Vista felt truly small, trapped beneath the weight of something far larger than itself.

A VISIT TO PREACHER'S POND

The snow kept falling, blanketing Bayou Vista in a silence so thick it felt like the town had been swallowed whole. The only sounds were the crunch of boots and the occasional murmur of wind through the trees. A small group moved purposefully toward Preacher's Pond, their breaths visible in the icy air, their steps heavy with trepidation.

Loretta led the way, her shoulders squared against the biting cold. Micky followed closely, his scarf pulled tight and his sharp gaze scanning the surroundings. Gail trailed slightly behind, her hands buried deep in her coat pockets, while Tricia and Taylor walked together, their whispers carrying hints of nervous energy. Shannon had joined them as they passed *Shanster Travels*, her bright red coat a pop of color against the muted whites and grays of the storm.

"Y'all really think we'll find something out here?" Taylor asked, her voice low but steady.

"It's worth a look," Loretta replied, her tone firm. "This is where Clara Mae and Emily were last seen. If there's any chance of finding answers, this is it."

Shannon caught up, adjusting her scarf against the cold. "Loretta, I've been thinking about what we found at the library yesterday. What do you make of it?"

Loretta slowed her pace, turning to glance at Shannon. Her breath clouded the air as she spoke. "What do you mean?"

Shannon's brow furrowed, her voice lowering. "Roy's name. You saw it, plain as day, in that journal. What do you think his involvement in all this could be? Or do you think he was involved at all?"

Loretta's jaw tightened as she looked ahead toward the pond. "I don't know. I want to believe he had nothing to do with Clara Mae, but... Roy was capable of anything. You know that as well as I do."

Shannon nodded, her voice hesitant. "He was a cruel man, no doubt about it. But there's a difference between cruelty and murdering a child."

Loretta stopped short, her boots crunching on the snow-covered ground. "He killed my mama, Shannon. Right in front of me at the old campground. And when they found Mary Campbell's body under that tree, everyone pointed the finger at him. Now, Clara Mae's name is in that journal right alongside his? How am I supposed to think that's just a coincidence?"

Micky, overhearing their conversation, turned to face them. "Coincidences, in my experience, are rarely as innocent as they seem. If his name's there, it's for a reason. The question is: what reason?"

Gail interjected, her voice laced with unease. "Or maybe folks just liked blaming him for everything that went wrong in this town. He was an easy target."

"Maybe," Loretta said, her tone softer now. "But if there's even a chance he was involved, I need to know. Clara Mae's family deserves to know."

Shannon adjusted her scarf and shivered. "Preacher's Pond gives me the creeps on a sunny day, let alone in the middle of a snowstorm."

"That's why we've got Micky," Tricia said with a grin, nudging him playfully. "He's the brave one, right?"

Micky chuckled softly, though his expression remained serious. "Bravery's got nothing to do with it, love. Curiosity, maybe. But places like this... they don't scare me. They intrigue me."

"That's because you're not from around here," Gail interjected, her voice carrying a nervous edge.

Taylor crossed her arms, glancing between Micky and the pond. "Not scared, huh? You might change your tune when the pond decides it doesn't like you poking around."

Micky smirked, tilting his head toward the frozen water. "I'd like to see it try. Places like this might not like strangers, but they tend to talk to them. You just have to know how to listen."

A sharp gust of wind swept past, sending snow swirling around their boots. The faint groan of the frozen pond echoed through the clearing, a sound that seemed to reverberate in their chests.

Shannon pulled her coat tighter and murmured, "If this place's got something to say, I don't wanna hear it."

Gail took a step back, her gaze fixed on the tree ahead. "Folks don't go near this place for a reason. Ain't just the stories—it's the feel of it."

Loretta's gaze drifted to the tree, her voice quieter now. "It's not just a feeling. It's like the ground here knows what happened and doesn't want us digging it up."

The group continued toward the pond, the tension between them as thick as the snow falling around them. As they neared the ancient oak, the atmosphere seemed to shift. The air grew colder, heavier, as though the world itself was holding its breath. The faint sound of cracking ice punctuated the quiet, a sharp, unnatural noise that made Tricia glance nervously at Taylor.

"Y'all heard that, right?" Tricia whispered, her tone uneasy.

Taylor nodded, her arms crossed tightly over her chest. "This whole place feels off. Like it's watching us."

The pond lay frozen, its surface shimmering faintly under the dull gray sky. Beyond it stood the ancient oak, its gnarled branches clawing at the air like skeletal fingers. At its base stood a simple wooden cross, weathered but still standing. Snow clung to its edges, giving it an almost ethereal glow.

"That tree's older than dirt," Taylor said, stopping short. "My granny used to tell stories about it. Said it's seen more than we ever will."

"Looks like it's seen better days too," Tricia muttered, eyeing the twisted trunk and snow-laden branches.

Loretta paused, her eyes fixed on the cross. Her voice softened. "That's where they found Mary Campbell."

Gail nodded, stepping closer. "Right there, under that tree. Folks said it was Roy who did it, but... well, Roy was blamed for a lot of things."

Loretta shook her head, the weight of her memories pressing down on her. "Blamed, sure. But he was guilty of plenty, too. My mama died because of him. And now, I can't help but wonder if Clara Mae and Emily did, too."

Micky crouched near the tree, brushing away the snow with his gloved hand. "Symbols like this," he murmured, his voice tinged with curiosity. "They're never random. Someone put it here for a reason."

Loretta knelt beside him, her breath clouding in the cold air. "You think it's connected to the disappearances?"

Micky tilted his head, his sharp blue eyes studying the worn carving. "It could be. Or it could be something older. Places like this, love—they have layers of history. Not all of it's pleasant."

"What do you mean?" Shannon asked, stepping closer.

"Places hold memories," Micky replied, his tone measured. "And sometimes, those memories seep into the land itself...like Devil's Marsh. I saw the symbol out there. You feel it, don't you? The weight of it."

Taylor shivered, wrapping her coat tighter around herself. "I feel like we're being watched."

"You're not wrong," Micky said quietly, his gaze fixed on the symbol. "This place—it's alive in its own way. And it's not happy."

Gail took a step back, her voice trembling. "Okay, that's enough. We've seen the tree, the cross, the pond. Let's go."

Loretta hesitated, her gaze lingering on the frozen surface of the pond. "If Roy was involved, we have to find out. Clara Mae's family deserves that much."

"Do you really think we'll get answers out here?" Shannon asked, her voice uncertain.

"If the pond doesn't tell us, something else will," Micky said, standing and brushing the snow from his gloves. "Secrets like this—they don't stay buried forever."

The group began their retreat, their footsteps crunching in the snow. As they passed the cross, Loretta's steps slowed. She turned back to the tree, her voice soft. "Mary didn't deserve what happened to her. None of them did."

"No, they didn't," Micky agreed, his tone somber. "But justice has a funny way of working. It doesn't always show up when you want it to."

Tricia glanced back toward the pond, her face pale. "I don't wanna see it if it does."

The snow fell heavier as they reached the edge of town, the soft glow of Christmas lights in the distance offering a small comfort. Shannon slowed, her gaze drifting back toward the pond. "Y'all feel like we left something behind?" she asked quietly.

Tricia shook her head. "I feel like something stayed behind. And I'm okay with that."

The group exchanged uneasy glances before continuing on. Behind them, the pond and the ancient tree stood silent and unmoving, as though watching, waiting, and remembering.

~ 19 ~

THE DREAM

Tanya's Crawfish Shack was bursting at the seams that evening. The storm outside raged on, blanketing the streets of Bayou Vista in even more snow, but inside, the warm glow of string lights and the scent of spicy gumbo created a haven for the townsfolk. Nearly everyone was there, gathered around tables and booths, trying to shake off the chill and share stories to pass the time.

The sounds of laughter, clinking bowls, and murmured conversations filled the room. Tanya herself was behind the counter, ladling steaming gumbo into bowls as fast as she could. Her cheeks were flushed, and her usual no-nonsense demeanor was softened by the holiday spirit that seemed to cling to the place despite the storm.

Loretta and Tricia sat together near the window, their table crowded with Gail, Patricia, and Margie, who had finally made it back from the airport with her brother Eddie. Firecracker was perched on a stool nearby, sharing her usual tall tales, while Micky leaned back in his chair, his scarf still wrapped loosely around his neck, sipping on a cup of hot tea. At the far end of the room, Rosie Fontenot and her best friend Gertie Landry were holding court, their voices cutting through the hum of conversation.

"Now, Gertie," Rosie drawled, her tone dripping with her usual dry humor. "If you're gonna tell the story, you might as well tell it right. Otherwise, you'll have half the town thinkin' you're crazier than me."

"Crazier than you?" Gertie shot back, adjusting her glasses. "That'd be a feat. But fine, I'll tell it right." She leaned forward, her voice lowering just enough to draw the attention of those nearby. "Y'all listen up, 'cause this ain't no ordinary story."

Loretta, curious as ever, turned her chair slightly. "What kind of story are we talking about?"

Gertie took a sip of sweet tea and set the glass down slowly, her eyes darting around the room. "It's about Mary Ellen White."

A hush fell over the nearby tables. Even Firecracker stopped mid-sentence, her usual grin fading. The name alone was enough to draw the room's collective attention.

Shannon, sitting across from Cindy Blevins and Taylor, frowned. "What about Mary?"

Gertie cleared her throat and leaned back in her chair, crossing her arms. "I had a dream about her last night."

Rosie rolled her eyes but smirked. "Oh, here we go. Gertie's gonna tell us she can see and talk to the dead, like Micky now."

"Shut it, Rosie," Gertie shot back, though there was no real bite in her words. "This ain't no regular dream, and you know it."

"Let her talk," Sheriff Emmett said from his seat near the counter, his deep voice cutting through the murmurs. "What'd you dream, Gertie?"

Gertie's gaze swept over the room, lingering on Micky, who nodded slightly, silently encouraging her to continue. She took a deep breath. "I saw her. Clear as day. She was standin' under that old tree by Preacher's Pond. She wasn't a little girl no more, but she still had her flaming red hair. She looked... older. Like she'd been waitin' a long time for someone to find her."

Micky set his coffee down, leaning forward. "And what was she doing, love?"

"She was callin' out," Gertie replied, her voice trembling slightly. "Not with words, exactly. But I could feel it, like she was pullin' me toward her. She wanted me to follow, to see somethin'."

"What did it feel like?" Loretta asked, her voice steady but tinged with unease.

"It was cold," Gertie whispered. "The kind of cold that sinks into your bones. And the air... it smelled sharp, like ice and somethin' else. Somethin' old. And when I stepped closer, I heard this sound—like a low hum, almost a heartbeat. It was comin' from the water. Then..."

Her voice faltered, and she gripped the edge of the table. "Then, I saw somethin' under the ice. It moved—slow and dark, like a shadow that wasn't just a shadow."

Rosie snorted, breaking the tension. "Probably wanted you to see where you left your common sense."

A few chuckles rippled through the room, but Loretta shot Rosie a look. "Rosie, hush. Let her finish."

Gertie ignored her friend's jab and continued. "She led me to the pond, right to the edge of the ice. And there, under the water... I saw her. Just for a moment. But she was there, lookin' up at me like she was tryin' to say somethin'. Her red hair floated around her face, and her eyes—they weren't scared. They were sad. Like she knew somethin' we don't."

The room fell silent, the weight of her words settling over everyone. Even Rosie seemed to lose her usual bravado, her smirk fading into something more subdued.

"What did you do?" Patricia asked, her voice barely above a whisper.

Gertie shook her head. "I woke up. But when I did, I swear I could still feel the cold from that water, like it'd seeped into my skin. And I ain't been able to shake the feelin' all day."

At a table nearby, Taylor fiddled nervously with her spoon, her eyes darting toward the window as though expecting to see Mary herself staring back. Firecracker leaned back in her chair, letting out a shaky laugh that didn't quite meet her eyes. "Sounds like you've been watching too many ghost stories, Gertie."

"Well, I ain't," Gertie snapped, though her tone softened. "I wish it was just a story. But it felt real. Too real."

"Dreams can be funny things," Eddie said, speaking up for the first time. His deep voice carried the same calmness as his sister Margie's. "Sometimes they're just dreams. But sometimes... they're something more."

"You believe her, then?" Cindy muttered, stirring her gumbo.

Eddie shrugged. "I've seen enough in my time to know the world's full of things we can't explain. And sometimes, those things reach out to us."

"Well, ain't that comforting," Cindy said under her breath.

Micky's voice broke through the chatter, steady and calm. "Dreams like that aren't uncommon in places like this. Land with history—especially troubled history—tends to hold onto its stories. And sometimes, it chooses someone to share them with."

"Why Gertie, then?" Taylor asked, her brow furrowing. "Why not... I don't know, someone closer to Mary?"

"Because I pay attention," Gertie said simply. "Maybe Mary knew I'd listen."

"She's been gone a long time," Gail said softly, her gaze distant. "But it feels like she's still here, doesn't it? Like she never really left."

Loretta nodded, her voice tight. "She's here, all right. And she's not the only one. This town's full of ghosts."

Rosie, ever the skeptic, leaned back in her chair. "Ghosts or not, what're we supposed to do about it? Ain't like we can just go out there and ask Mary what she wants."

"Maybe we don't have to," Micky said, his tone thoughtful. "Sometimes, the answers come to us when we least expect them. We just have to be willing to see them."

"Well, I don't wanna see nothing," Tricia said, shivering despite the warmth of the room. "I just wanna finish my gumbo and forget about ponds and trees and... whatever this is."

The room erupted in nervous laughter, the tension easing slightly. Tanya appeared from behind the counter, wiping her hands on her apron. "Y'all are spooking yourselves half to death. Eat your gumbo and leave the ghosts to the folks who ain't got better sense to be scared of them."

"You talkin' about me?" Micky asked, his eyes twinkling with humor.

"If the shoe fits," Tanya shot back, grinning.

The group settled back into their meals, the buzz of conversation picking up again. But beneath the laughter and chatter, an undercurrent of unease remained, threading through the room like a silent specter.

As the night wore on, the gumbo bowls emptied, and the snow continued to fall. Yet, in the hearts of those who'd heard Gertie's tale, the cold stayed, lingering like a whisper waiting to be heard. And somewhere out there, beyond the warmth of the shack, Preacher's Pond waited, its secrets buried but not forgotten.

~ 20 ~

ON THE NINTH NIGHT...

The next morning, the snowstorm had calmed, leaving Bayou Vista blanketed in snow so pristine it could've been on a postcard. The town sparkled under the weak sunlight, but the storm had left more than snow behind. Despite the icy streets, *Bayou Bliss Coffee House*, buzzed with warmth and conversation. Twinkling Christmas lights wrapped around the windows, and the faint scent of pine from a small tree in the corner added a holiday charm. But beneath the festive cheer lingered an unease that no one could quite shake.

Firecracker sat at her usual spot by the window. Her bright yellow scarf and patched denim jacket were as bold as her personality. She leaned forward, elbows on the table, daring anyone to pass without stopping for a word.

At the counter, Micky Vermooch sat with his coffee, the steam curling up toward his face. His English accent and mysterious presence made him an outsider to some, but he had earned the town's trust, and his shop, *Micky's*

Magical Things, was a beloved curiosity. Every so often, his gaze flicked toward the window, his expression thoughtful, as though expecting something—or someone.

Behind the counter, Brenda moved effortlessly, sliding mugs of coffee and plates of beignets to regulars. The faint hum of a Christmas carol played on the radio until it suddenly cut off, leaving an eerie silence that seemed to seep into the room. Brenda frowned, tapping the side of it, but no sound came.

Loretta, Shannon, and Tricia huddled at a nearby table. Their voices were low, but it was clear their conversation circled back to Gertie Landry's haunting dream from the night before—a tale that had left the whole town on edge.

Firecracker's smirk faltered for a moment as her eyes wandered to the frosted window. A figure moved past—a fleeting shadow, gone almost as quickly as it appeared. Her stomach tightened, but she shook it off, pulling her scarf tighter around her neck.

"Wind's playing tricks," she muttered to herself, though her tone lacked conviction.

Brenda caught her eye. "You see something?"

Firecracker hesitated, then shrugged. "Probably nothing. Just the snow messing with the light."

The door jingled, letting in a sharp gust of cold air as Patricia, Gail, and Margie stomped in.

"Good Lord, it's colder than a freezer full of crawfish out there," Patricia said, rubbing her hands together.

Margie unwrapped her scarf and raised an amused eyebrow, her lips curling into a playful smirk. "You hogging the table for gossip, or can we sit with you?"

Firecracker smiled, pushing her unease aside. "Pull up a chair, but don't think for a second I won't spill if there's something juicy."

Brenda placed steaming mugs of coffee in front of the newcomers before they even asked. "Y'all look half-froze. Sit yourselves down and thaw out."

Gail cradled her mug like it was life itself. "What's the talk this morning? Feels like the whole town's got something to say."

Firecracker leaned back, her tone playful but with a flicker of unease. "Buzz? Honey, it's more like a roar. Gertie's dream sent folks straight to prayer last night, and now folks are saying they felt something watching them."

Patricia frowned. "Watching? What kind of watching?"

Margie's voice dropped, her unease evident. "People said they felt eyes on them, even when they were alone. One woman swears she heard footsteps outside her house during the storm. Her husband went out this morning—didn't see a thing."

Brenda paused mid-wipe of the counter. "You think someone's sneaking around? Or something else?"

Firecracker waved a hand, brushing it off. "If someone was watching me, I hope they enjoyed the show. I don't scare easy."

Micky's voice cut through, smooth and deliberate. "Sometimes, it's not the shadows you see that you should fear. It's the ones that hide in plain sight. In places like this, the past doesn't stay buried. It doesn't rest—it waits."

Firecracker raised an eyebrow, her smirk faltering again. "Well, ain't you just full of holiday cheer, Micky."

He gave her a small, knowing smile. "Just calling it like I see it."

Before anyone could respond, a faint knock echoed through the room. Everyone froze, their eyes darting toward the window. Brenda stepped forward, her voice trembling slightly. "Probably just the wind hitting the Christmas decorations on the window."

No one responded, and the tension only grew thicker.

The door jingled again, and Sheriff Emmett walked in. His face was drawn, his shoulders heavy as he brushed snow from his coat.

"Morning Sheriff," Brenda called, pouring him a fresh cup. "You look like you've been up all night. Coffee's on me."

"Much obliged," Emmett said, taking a stool at the counter. He warmed his hands on the mug before speaking, his voice grave. "Firecracker, I need a word."

The room went still. Firecracker leaned forward, her tone skeptical but curious. "Me? What for?"

"I got a call from your neighbor this morning. They said there was a package wrapped in brown paper—just like the others—sitting on your porch. You didn't notice it?"

"No," Firecracker replied, shaking her head. "I always go through the back to get to the garage."

Emmett leaned forward slightly. "Did you see or hear anything unusual last night?"

Firecracker frowned, her thoughts spinning. "I went to bed early. What kinda something are we talking about?"

Emmett reached into his coat and pulled out a tattered diary. Its edges were burned, the cover warped, and the pages smelled faintly of mildew, as though it had been hidden somewhere damp and forgotten. He set it on the counter.

"This was on your porch. Pages were scattered all over. Recognize it?"

Firecracker's eyes widened, her breath catching. "That's... that's my old diary. The one I lost when we moved. How in the world..."

Her fingers hovered above the diary but didn't touch it. Memories surged forward—Christmas mornings with her parents before the divorce, the smell of pine and the crackle of a fireplace as they laughed and opened presents. She'd written about those moments in that diary, back when life felt perfect. She clenched her fists and pulled her hand back.

Patricia reached over, placing a comforting hand on her arm. "You okay, hon?"

Firecracker nodded, but her voice was quieter now. "Yeah, it's just... that diary's from years ago. I wrote down everything back then. My dreams, my plans... before life got complicated."

Micky stood, his gaze fixed on the diary. He hesitated, then reached out to touch it. His hand hovered above the cover for a moment, and when he finally made contact, his expression darkened.

"Whoever left this for you wasn't just dropping off a book, love," he said softly. "They were leaving a message."

Firecracker snapped her head toward him, her voice sharp. "What kinda message?"

Micky's voice softened, but his tone was grave. "Maybe it's time to face what you've been avoiding. The past doesn't stay buried in places like this. It finds its way back—always."

The faint sound of church bells echoed in the distance, their haunting chime cutting through the silence. Brenda, still at the counter, glanced toward the window. Her voice was barely above a whisper. "Did anyone else hear the wind last night? It sounded like... laughing."

And on Firecracker's porch, the footprints leading away from her door stopped abruptly—vanishing as if they had never been there.

Somewhere in Bayou Vista, the Watcher waited. Hidden in plain sight, it left no tracks, yet saw everything. The diary was just another message—a chilling reminder that more was yet to come.

~ 21 ~

CONFRONTING THE PAST

The warm hum of chatter in *Bayou Bliss Coffee House* was interrupted as the door swung open with a loud jingle. A sharp gust of cold air followed Rosie Fontenot and Gertie Landry as they burst inside, their faces flushed, not just from the cold but from sheer panic.

The room froze. Firecracker, perched at her usual table, leaned forward, her yellow scarf slipping off one shoulder. Brenda, steady as a rock on most days, jerked the coffee pot, spilling a trail of dark liquid across the counter. Sheriff Emmett, who had just taken a sip of his coffee, set his cup down with deliberate calm, his sharp eyes narrowing on the two women.

"Sheriff!" Rosie's voice cracked, loud and high-pitched, as she shoved her way through the tables. "You gotta come quick!"

Gertie, pale as the frost-covered trees outside, clutched her scarf close to her chest. "It's Joe and Helen, Sheriff. They're gone! Something bad's happened."

"Gone?" Patricia's voice cut through the air. She set her coffee down hard, the ceramic cup rattling against the saucer. "What do you mean gone?"

"They ain't just up and left," Rosie snapped, her hands fluttering in front of her. "Their front door's wide open, and there's blood everywhere—walls, floor, even the porch steps—but not a soul in sight!"

Brenda, uncharacteristically shaky, turned to Gertie. "Blood? Are you sure, Rosie? Not just something spilled? Maybe... maybe Joe dropped something from hunting."

Rosie shot her a look that could've frozen the bayou. "Does this look like a time to be rational, Brenda? It's blood. Real blood. The smell of it was enough to churn my stomach."

Gertie nodded, her voice trembling. "I was knockin' on their door to bring 'em cookies—Joe loves my sugar cookies, y'know—but when I stepped on the porch, there it was. Bright red, Sheriff. And it smelled..." Her face crumpled, and she buried it in her scarf. "It smelled awful."

The coffee shop erupted in hushed whispers. Margie muttered a prayer under her breath. Firecracker stood up, her usual sass replaced by genuine concern.

Across the room, Evelyn from *Frog's Delight Bakery* dropped her fork onto her plate of beignets with a sharp clatter. "Blood on the porch?" she whispered to LaDonna, her voice shaking. "What in God's name is happening to this town?"

Mr. Dupree, standing near the counter, dropped his keys with a clink and bent to retrieve them, muttering, "You reckon we should start lockin' our doors, Brenda?"

The tension thickened as Brenda snapped at him. "Maybe you should. Now sit down, Mr. Dupree, or go on home. We've got enough worrying folks here already."

His face flushed, and he quickly backed away, muttering, "Didn't mean nothin' by it..."

Emmett rose slowly, his chair scraping against the floor. "Calm down, now. Take a breath and tell me what you're talking about."

Rosie's voice climbed higher. "Calm? Calm? Their house looks like a damn crime scene, and you're tellin' me to calm down?"

"Easy now," Firecracker interjected, stepping between Rosie and the sheriff. "Let the man do his job."

Emmett nodded to Firecracker before turning back to Brenda. "Call the deputy. Tell him to meet me at Joe and Helen's place. Rosie, Gertie, sit yourselves down and catch your breath."

"Catch our breath?" Rosie snapped. "You need to be out there, findin' out what the hell's goin' on!"

"I'll get there," Emmett said, his tone steady, though his eyes betrayed the weight of the moment. "Now sit."

Micky stood, setting his coffee cup down gently. "Sheriff, if you don't mind, I'd like to join you."

Emmett raised an eyebrow. "Are you sure, Micky?"

"I have a knack for seeing things others miss," Micky said evenly, his English accent cutting through the room's growing tension. "And if blood's involved, I'd wager you could use a fresh set of eyes."

Firecracker stepped forward. "Sheriff, you sure you don't need more hands? This sounds serious."

Emmett shook his head firmly. "Appreciate the offer, but this ain't a job for just anyone. Y'all stay put and keep things steady here. Micky, let's go."

The sheriff's truck crunched to a halt outside the Smiths' home. The modest clapboard house, adorned with sagging Christmas lights, looked ordinary except for the front door, which swung ajar in the wind. Blood stained the snow on the porch steps, smeared across the doorframe in streaks.

"Good Lord," Emmett muttered as he stepped out of the truck, his boots sinking into the snow. "Stay close, Micky. And don't touch nothing."

Micky followed, his gaze sharp. "Wouldn't dream of it, Sheriff."

Inside, the house was steeped in an oppressive silence. The metallic tang of blood hit them immediately, mingling with the faint aroma of cinnamon and pine from holiday candles still burning. The living room was a wreck. Furniture overturned, a lamp shattered on the floor, and blood spattered across the walls like a twisted piece of art.

"This wasn't random," Micky said softly, crouching by a bloodstain near the sofa. His fingers hovered above it, careful not to touch. "This doesn't feel like anger—it feels like intent."

"Intent?" Emmett repeated, his voice tight. "You saying this ain't human?"

Micky looked up, his face grim. "I'm saying whoever—or whatever—did this had a purpose. Look at the spray, the streaks. Someone was dragged."

"Dragged where?" Emmett asked.

The trail of blood led down the hallway to the back door, which hung open slightly. Snow had blown in, but outside, the pristine blanket of white was undisturbed.

"That doesn't make sense," Emmett muttered, stepping onto the porch. "If they were dragged out, there'd be tracks."

"Unless they didn't leave by the door," Micky said, his tone chillingly calm.

The faintest creak echoed from upstairs. Both men froze. Emmett's hand instinctively went to his holster.

"You hear that?" Emmett whispered.

Micky nodded, his eyes scanning the shadowed staircase. "Could be the wind. Or..."

"Or what?"

Micky met his gaze, unflinching. "Or something waiting."

The two men exchanged a tense glance before the creak came again, this time louder. Emmett motioned for Micky to stay back as he crept toward the stairs. Each step groaned under his weight, the sound amplified by the thick silence of the house. When he reached the top, the hallway was empty.

Behind him, Micky called up, his voice low. "Sheriff, things like this don't stop. They just wait for the right moment to start again."

Emmett's jaw clenched. He turned back to the staircase and descended, his movements deliberate.

Back at *Bayou Bliss Coffee House*— the tension in the coffee shop hadn't eased. Rosie sat hunched over her cup of coffee, her hands trembling. Gertie kept her eyes glued to the window, as though expecting Joe and Helen to walk down the street.

Firecracker tapped her foot impatiently, her arms crossed. "What's taking them so long? They should've called by now."

Patricia leaned closer to Gail. "You think this has anything to do with that diary and the other gifts?"

"Or the laughing in the wind," Brenda added softly, her face pale. "I swear, last night... it sounded like a child."

Rosie looked up sharply. "Child? No, but I heard knockin'. Faint, like someone tappin' on my back door. Didn't see anyone, though."

The room fell silent again, the unease heavy in the air.

Back at the *Smith house*—on the back porch, Emmett and Micky stood staring at the untouched snow. The silence was broken only by the distant whistle of the wind.

"What now?" Emmett asked, his voice low.

Micky didn't answer immediately. He tilted his head, listening.

Then it came. A faint, melodic hum—almost like a lullaby—drifting through the air.

Emmett stiffened. "You hear that?"

Micky nodded, his expression unreadable. "We wait," he said finally. "And we prepare. Because this isn't over. Not by a long shot."

Emmett glanced at him, his jaw tightening. "We'll figure it out. Whatever it is."

But deep down, even he wasn't sure he believed that.

A TOWN ON EDGE

Bayou Bliss Coffee House had never been this crowded. It felt like the entire town of Bayou Vista had crammed itself into the small, warmly lit space. The rich smell of Brenda's fresh coffee and the faint scent of pine from the Christmas decorations were drowned out by the thick air of fear and speculation.

Brenda moved behind the counter like a woman on a mission, refilling coffee mugs and delivering plates of beignets, though her usual cheer had vanished. Her hands shook slightly as she set down a mug in front of Firecracker, who was sitting at her usual table; the bright yellow scarf sat crooked around her neck.

"Y'all really think Joe and Helen are... gone gone?" Brenda asked, her voice low but shaky.

Firecracker, her usual confidence dimmed, glanced at the door for the hundredth time. "Gone, missing, or worse. Sheriff'll tell us when he gets back, but from what Rosie and Gertie said, it doesn't sound good."

The room buzzed with nervous energy, snippets of conversation flying from every corner.

"I heard there was blood everywhere," muttered Taylor, her hand clutching her coffee cup so tightly her knuckles were white.

LaDonna from *Frog's Delight Bakery* nodded solemnly. "Blood and no tracks. That doesn't make a lick of sense."

The door jingled, and every head in the room turned as one. The silence that followed was so heavy you could hear the soft hum of the coffee machine behind the counter. Sheriff Emmett stepped inside, snow dusting his shoulders, followed by Micky, his expression unreadable as always.

"You better talk, Sheriff," barked Mr. Lucky, one of the old-timers sitting by the Christmas tree with Shannon. "What happened out there?"

The tension in the room snapped as people started talking over one another.

"Is Joe okay?"

"What about Helen?"

"Is it true there are no tracks in the snow?"

Emmett held up a hand, his voice firm. "Quiet down now! Everyone calm yourselves. Let me talk."

The murmurs faded, though the atmosphere remained electric. Emmett glanced at Brenda, who handed him a fresh cup of coffee without a word. He took a long sip before speaking.

"We didn't find Joe or Helen," Emmett said, his voice steady but grim. "There's blood, plenty of it, but no signs of them. No tracks are leading out. It's like they vanished."

The room erupted again, louder this time. Rosie Fontenot, seated near the counter, buried her face in her hands. "Vanished? How in the hell does someone just disappear like that?"

"Exactly!" Mr. Lucky shouted, pointing a finger in the air. "This ain't the first time somethin' like this happened. Y'all remember Mary Ellen White back in '48?"

"Don't start with that nonsense," snapped Mr. Dupree, his weathered face drawn tight. "Ain't nobody wants to dredge up them old ghosts."

"I'll dredge 'em up," Lucky shot back. "Mary Ellen disappeared in the middle of a snowstorm, just like this, and you know what the town did? They made promises to her family to 'look the other way.' Did favors for them to keep them quiet."

The room fell eerily silent. Even Brenda stopped moving, her hands frozen mid-air. Gertie leaned forward, her voice breaking the quiet. "And what about Clara Mae and Emily Carr, thirty years later? Same damn thing. Everyone is pretending it didn't happen. Y'all think this is connected?"

Loretta, seated at a table with Gail and Tricia, spoke up, her voice trembling. "What if it isn't about the girls from the snowstorm from the past? What if this is about all the women who've gone missing over the years? Like the ones all of you blamed on Roy?"

The mention of Roy, the man the town had long believed responsible for several disappearances, sent a shiver through the room. Shannon shook her head, her voice a near whisper. "Roy's dead."

"Or maybe," Loretta continued, her voice stronger now, "it's the serial killer from *Devil's Marsh.* What if he's still alive? What if he's the Watcher?"

The already tense room boiled over.

"You don't think—" LaDonna began, her voice shaking. "No, that can't be. That killer's dead. Has to be."

"Dead?" Rosie blurted, her voice high-pitched with hysteria. "Dead? Y'all thought Roy was the one behind those missin' women, but what if we were wrong about all of it? What if it's someone—or somethin'—that's been here all along?"

A wave of unease swept through the coffee shop. People shifted in their seats, avoiding each other's eyes. Mayor Steve, who had been sitting quietly by the window, suddenly stood up, his face red with anger.

"There ain't no damn serial killer in Devil's Marsh!" he shouted, pointing a finger at Micky. "You took care of that, didn't you, Micky? Didn't you and Preacher John handle it?"

All eyes turned to Micky, whose calm demeanor didn't falter. He took a sip of coffee, his movements deliberate, before setting the cup down. "Handle it, Mayor?" His rich English accent carried a cool edge. "I may have dealt with certain... matters in the Marsh, but as for what's truly out there? Some things can't be handled. Some things wait."

The weight of his words pressed down on the room. The mayor opened his mouth to respond but faltered, sinking back into his seat with a heavy sigh.

"Wait for what?" Patricia asked, her voice cutting through the silence. "For more people to disappear? For someone to finally figure out what the hell's going on?"

Before Micky could reply, Deputy Wade burst through the door, his face pale as a sheet. The room collectively inhaled, bracing for more bad news.

"Sheriff," Wade said, barely above a whisper. "We got another one. Over by Devil's Marsh."

The room erupted again, chaos breaking out as people shouted over one another. Brenda banged a spoon on the counter, shouting for quiet.

Micky stood, his eyes narrowing. "Another one? Who?"

"Donna Lou," Wade said, his voice cracking. "Same thing. Blood everywhere. No tracks. Just... gone."

Micky's expression darkened, and he turned to Emmett. "Sheriff, I think it's time we had a proper look at that Marsh."

Emmett nodded, his jaw tight. "Let's go."

"Wait!" Tanya called out, her voice trembling. "Before you go, Wade, did you see anything? Hear anything strange?"

Wade hesitated, his face pale. "There was... something," he admitted finally. "A hum. Faint, like... like someone was singing. And the smell—like ashes. But the air was still. No fire anywhere."

The murmurs in the room grew louder. Firecracker clutched her scarf tighter. "Hummin'? You sure?"

Wade nodded. "I swear it. Never heard nothin' like it before."

The door swung shut behind Emmett and Micky, leaving the coffee shop in stunned silence. The melodic sound of a Christmas carol playing faintly from the radio seemed painfully out of place.

Cindy, from *C&D Kwik Stop*, leaned toward Brenda, her voice barely above a whisper. "You ever wonder if maybe this town's got something to answer for? Something we can't bury no more?"

Brenda didn't answer. She just stared at the door, her hands shaking as she gripped the edge of the counter.

Outside, the snow fell heavier, blanketing Bayou Vista in a silence that felt anything but peaceful.

~ 23 ~

ON THE TENTH NIGHT...

The sheriff's truck cut through the snow-covered backroads of Bayou Vista, its tires crunching in the stillness. Sheriff Emmett kept his hands tight on the wheel, his jaw set in a way that warned against small talk. Beside him, Micky Vermooch sat with his coffee gone cold in his travel mug, his gaze fixed out the passenger window.

"Sheriff," Micky finally said, breaking the silence. His voice was measured, his English accent crisp, though there was a weariness behind it. "There's something I've not shared about the Marsh. It's time you knew."

Emmett glanced at him briefly before returning his focus to the road. "Now's as good a time as any, I reckon. Go on."

Micky shifted in his seat, choosing his words carefully. "Billy and his sister had a son, Micah. He would be around fifty years old now if he's still alive."

"Micah," Emmett repeated, tasting the name as if it were a bitter pill. "Didn't know Billy had a son."

"Few people do," Micky said. "It wasn't something folks were eager to talk about back then. Born out of—" He paused, choosing his words carefully. "A complicated situation. Billy's sister, the boy's mother, took her own life shortly after he was born. From what I've pieced together, Billy hid the baby in the marsh because his mother had threatened to kill him—sacrifice him to the marsh. The child disappeared into the wilderness, raised by no one yet shaped by everyone in whispers and fear."

Emmett frowned, his grip tightening on the wheel. "And you're telling me this now because…?"

"Because I think Micah's still out there," Micky admitted, his voice barely above a whisper. "I banished the demon that haunted Billy's house and the land, but Micah? He's human. Whatever's been surviving out there all these years has been watching—learning. I still have a camera hidden in the marsh from when Izzy was there, and every night, I review the footage, searching for any sign of him. But lately, there's been nothing. I didn't want to stir up panic—especially not during the holidays—but everything went quiet after I dealt with that demon. Until now."

"You're saying you think Micah might be the Watcher?" Emmett asked, his tone skeptical but not dismissive.

Micky hesitated, then shook his head. "I don't know. Could be him, could be something else. A ghost from the past, perhaps. What I do know is this—it's no coincidence all this is happening again."

The truck hit a pothole, jolting them both. Emmett steadied the wheel, letting out a slow breath. "You did the right thing, not telling the town. They would have lost their minds." He shook his head, his grip tightening on the wheel. "I thought this town was finally free of that entire deranged bloodline of the LaBlancs. I can't believe that sick clown killer had a child."

"They're already on edge," Micky said, his voice tinged with regret. "But now, with these disappearances and gifts, I don't think we have the luxury of secrets anymore."

Emmett nodded, his eyes narrowing as the snow began to fall heavier. "Let's just see what the Marsh has to say, if anything."

When they returned to town, the chaos they had left behind had only multiplied. The parking lot of the sheriff's office was packed, cars parked haphazardly in the snow. A mob of townsfolk had gathered outside, their voices carrying into the cold night.

As soon as Emmett and Micky stepped out of the truck, they were swarmed.

"Sheriff, what happened to Donna Lou?" shouted Margie, her voice strained with worry.

"What about Joe and Helen?" Rosie Fontenot added, clutching a shawl tight around her shoulders.

"Are we dealin' with a serial killer or what?" bellowed Mr. Lucky, who stood at the edge of the crowd like a self-appointed spokesperson.

"Quiet down!" Emmett barked, raising his hands to calm the crowd. "One at a time, for the love of God."

The crowd didn't settle. The questions only grew louder, overlapping in a cacophony of fear and speculation.

LaDonna stepped forward, her apron dusted with flour. "Sheriff, people are scared. They need answers."

"I understand that," Emmett said, his voice firm but steady. "But y'all crowding the office like this ain't helping. Go home. I'll call a town meeting tomorrow."

"That ain't soon enough!" snapped Cindy Blevins. "Donna Lou's missing, and Joe and Helen too. What if we're next?"

Before Emmett could respond, Stephanie Terry, the nail technician from Bayou Belle Beauty, pushed her way through the crowd, clutching a brown paper package. Her face was pale, her breathing ragged.

"Sheriff," she gasped, thrusting the package toward him. "This was on my porch. I... I didn't open it."

Emmett took the package, his heart sinking as he recognized the familiar brown paper tied with twine. The crowd fell silent as he untied the string and carefully unwrapped it. Inside was a single candle, its wick blackened and snuffed out. He held it up for everyone to see.

"What does it mean?" Stephanie whispered, tears brimming in her eyes.

Micky stepped closer, his expression grim. "A life taken too soon. That's what it means."

The crowd erupted in panic.

"A candle? What the hell does that mean for the rest of us?" shouted Tanya.

"It's a message," Micky said, his voice calm but cutting through the noise. "The Watcher's leaving us a message."

"Message my ass!" Dondi snapped, his voice trembling. "This ain't no message—it's a warning!"

Emmett held up his hands again, his voice booming over the chaos. "Enough! Y'all need to calm down. We're investigating this, and I swear to you, we'll find out who's behind it."

"That's what you said about Roy," muttered someone in the back of the crowd.

"And Roy's dead!" Firecracker shouted, stepping forward. "Y'all need to stop blaming him for every damn thing that happens in this town."

"Then who do we blame?" demanded Taylor. "Because someone's taking people, and it sure as hell ain't random!"

Loretta's voice cut through the noise, trembling but clear. "What if it's the killer of Devil's Marsh? What if he's come back to finish what started years ago?"

The crowd turned to Micky, their eyes full of questions and accusations. The mayor pointed a finger at him. "You told us there weren't no danger in Devil's Marsh. You said you took care of it!"

Micky met his gaze evenly, his tone measured but firm. "I took care of the demon. I didn't say the Marsh itself was done taking lives."

The weight of his words hung in the air, heavy and suffocating.

Catrina stepped forward, breaking the silence. "Sheriff, what do we do now? We can't just sit around waiting for the next package to show up."

Emmett glanced at Micky, then back at the crowd. "Y'all go home. Lock your doors. Stay in pairs if you can. Don't let anyone in you don't trust. And if you see something—anything—call us."

"But what about Donna Lou?" The Judge asked, his voice breaking. "What about Joe and Helen?"

"We'll find them," Emmett said firmly. "I promise you that."

As the crowd slowly began to disperse, Firecracker lingered near Brenda, her arms crossed tightly over her chest. "You think it's over? You think he's done?"

Brenda shook her head, her voice barely above a whisper. "No. I think it's just starting."

Outside, the snow continued to fall, soft and relentless, muffling the sound of the crowd as they left. From somewhere in the distance, a faint hum drifted on the wind, so quiet it could have been imagined—or not.

WHO IS THAT?

The frost clung stubbornly to the windows of *Bayou Bliss Coffee House*, the swirling snow outside painting a muted, dreamlike scene. Inside, Brenda hummed a soft rendition of "Silent Night," her voice trembling slightly as she refilled mugs with coffee that seemed darker and heavier than usual. Despite the holiday lights strung around the shop and the faint scent of cinnamon rolls, the air inside felt stifling, weighed down by fear.

Micky sat near the window, his steaming cup of coffee untouched. His sharp blue eyes flitted between the townsfolk, their hushed conversations and darting glances over their shoulders speaking louder than words. Across from him, Loretta nervously fidgeted with a sugar packet, tearing it into tiny pieces.

"I can feel it, Micky," Loretta muttered, her voice barely above a whisper. "Like something's about to happen."

Micky nodded, his gaze shifting to the snow-covered street outside. "Fear changes people, Loretta. Makes them see shadows where there are none—and miss the ones that matter."

At the counter, LaDonna leaned forward, her arms crossed tightly as she spoke to Brenda. "You hear anything more about Nancy?"

Brenda sighed, setting a plate of untouched cookies back on the counter. "Not a word. Sheriff's working on it, but... Lord, LaDonna, how's a woman like Nancy just vanish?"

"She doesn't," LaDonna said firmly. "Someone made her vanish, and whoever did it's going to regret it. This town doesn't take kindly to its own being messed with."

Rosie, seated at a nearby table with Patricia and Tanya, raised her voice. "I'm tellin' y'all, this ain't random. First Joe and Helen, then Donna Lou, and now Nancy? Four people in less than 24 hours! Someone's out there watchin' us. Mark my words." She leaned forward, her tone dropping just enough to make the others lean in too. "And they're all senior citizens, just like me and Gertie. You think that's a coincidence? 'Cause I don't."

Patricia trembled as she clutched a handkerchief in her lap, her knuckles white. "Nancy's my neighbor," she said, her voice breaking. "She was baking gingerbread yesterday. She said she would bring some by this morning. What if she's out there now, cold and alone?" Her words dissolved into a soft sob as she pressed the handkerchief to her face.

Rosie reached over and patted Patricia's shoulder, though her own voice carried a sharp edge. "Don't you start thinkin' like that. Nancy's tougher than she looks. But I'll be damned if we let this town fall apart over this."

Tanya leaned in, lowering her voice. "You think this has anything to do with Devil's Marsh? Folks say it's got a way of bringing out the worst in people."

Shannon, overhearing, set down her coffee cup with a clatter. "Mama used to say the Marsh has a way of calling folks back, whether they're ready or not. But let's not add fuel to the fire, Tanya. This town's scared enough."

By late morning, *St. Theresa's Church* was packed wall-to-wall. Snow fell steadily outside, muffling the usual hum of the town, but inside, the sanctuary hummed with tension. Pine wreaths adorned the walls, and flickering candles cast long, dancing shadows across the pews. The soft hum of a child singing "Jingle Bells" drifted through the crowd before a parent hushed them, the joyful tune cut short by a worried glance.

Sheriff Emmett stood at the front, flanked by Preacher John. His voice cut through the murmurs as he raised his hand for quiet. "All right, y'all. I know you're scared, and I know you're angry. But we need to keep calm while we figure this out."

In the second row, Cindy Blevins nudged Melissa Staggs with her elbow. "Do you see that man by the door?"

Melissa frowned, following Cindy's gaze. "What man?"

Cindy tilted her head slightly. "Back there. The one in the coat. Don't think I've ever seen him before."

Melissa finally spotted him, her eyes widening. "Well, I'll be. He's something, ain't he?"

The man stood casually near the door, his long black coat dusted with snow and a scarf draped loosely around his neck. His dark hair was slicked back, and his sharp features caught the dim light in a way that made him almost seem to glow. But there was something else—an antique pin on his lapel, a weathered cameo that seemed both out of place and strangely familiar.

"He looks familiar," Tanya whispered, leaning toward Patricia. "Like someone I've seen before... but that's impossible."

Patricia shivered, stealing a quick glance over her shoulder before snapping her attention forward. "Don't start with that, Tanya. Not here. Not now." She tried to lighten the mood with a nervous giggle. "Besides, he's kinda cute."

Micky, standing near the side aisle with Shannon and Brenda, noticed the shift in the room. Whispers buzzed like static, heads turning one by one toward the back of the sanctuary. He leaned closer to Brenda, keeping his voice low. "What's got everyone so distracted?"

Brenda gestured subtly with her chin. "That man. By the door."

Micky turned slightly, his gaze scanning the crowd, but before he could catch a glimpse, the faint creak of the church door cut through the murmurs. The man was gone.

Shannon whispered, "He looked familiar, Micky. Not like someone I know now—like someone from a picture or something. You ever get that feeling?"

Micky's jaw tightened. "I didn't see him. But I'd wager he wasn't here by accident."

At the front, Emmett's voice rose, pulling the attention back to him. "We've had disappearances," he said, his tone steady but grim. "And I know y'all want answers. So do I. My deputies and I are following every lead, but I need everyone to stay vigilant. Stay in pairs, lock your doors, and if you see anything—anything at all—you call us."

Patricia clutched the pew in front of her, her voice breaking. "Nancy's my neighbor, Sheriff. She's family. What are y'all doing to bring her back?"

Rosie stood as well, her voice rising. "What Patricia's saying is what we're all feeling. This town's been through enough. We need answers, Emmett. We can't just sit around waiting for someone else to vanish."

"I understand, Rosie," Emmett said, meeting her gaze. "And we're doing everything we can."

Tanya spoke up from the back, her voice trembling. "But how do we know we're safe? How do we know this won't happen again?"

"You don't," Micky interjected, stepping forward slightly. His calm voice cut through the tension like a blade. "But fear is their weapon. If we let it control us, we've already lost. Unity is ours. Stay together, stay watchful, and don't let panic take root."

His words seemed to resonate, the murmurs quieting. Preacher John clasped his hands together. "Let us not forget the season we're in, y'all. This is a time of hope, of light overcoming darkness. We'll get through this together."

As the meeting wound down, Cindy and Melissa lingered near the door, their gazes fixed on the snow-covered street. "You think he's still out there?" Cindy asked softly.

Melissa shook her head. "I don't know. But I don't like it, Cindy. Not one bit."

Brenda glanced at Micky, who stood on the steps of the church, his sharp gaze fixed on the horizon. The snow fell heavier, muffling the town's sounds. Brenda handed him a scarf, breaking the silence. "You all right?"

Micky didn't answer immediately. He stared into the growing white abyss, his thoughts a jumble of suspicion and unease. *Was the Marsh calling someone back—or was something else at play?*

The wind shifted suddenly, carrying a faint sound—a crunch of footsteps, perhaps, or just the whisper of the Marsh. Whatever it was, it left Micky with a single, unshakable thought: *Bayou Vista wasn't ready.*

~ 25 ~

ON THE ELEVENTH NIGHT...

The icy wind howled outside Tanya's Crawfish Shack, rattling the windows as if it sought to claw its way in. Inside, the townsfolk huddled together, their voices lively, though an unspoken tension coiled beneath the surface. The scent of gumbo and crawfish étouffée mingled with the crisp tang of pine garlands strung around the room, but even the cheerful blink of Christmas lights couldn't fully chase away the unease hanging in the air.

Tanya leaned on the counter, her red apron dusted with flour, as she exchanged lively whispers with Patricia and Shannon seated at a nearby table.

"Well, I'll say it again," Patricia said, her eyes bright with a mix of nerves and curiosity. "That man at the meeting—he had a presence, didn't he? It's like he'd stepped out of one of those old movies. Dark and mysterious. And that coat—oh, that coat!"

Motioning toward Gerald at the next table, Shannon smirked, cradling her mug of sweet tea. "Don't let Gerald hear you say that, Patricia. He might just stop putting up those Christmas lights out of spite. You know that man is sweet on you."

Tanya chuckled as she adjusted a wreath above the counter, the motion mechanical, as if she were trying to distract herself. "Y'all keep going on about his coat. Did nobody else notice that pin he was wearing? The old cameo?"

"Yes!" Patricia's voice rose, drawing a few glances. "It looked antique. Like something that didn't belong on a man—almost like it wasn't his to begin with."

The faint sound of silverware clinking against plates filled the silence that followed. At a table in the corner, Gertie leaned in close to Rosie, her voice a conspiratorial hiss. "I'm tellin' you, it's gotta be Krampus."

Rosie, mid-sip of her coffee, choked, barely stifling a snort. "Gertie, you've officially lost your last marble. Krampus? Really? He comes for kids. What makes you think he's decided to switch to the senior circuit?"

"Why not?" Gertie shot back, her tone dead serious. "Look at who's vanished—Nancy, Donna Lou, Joe, Helen—all older than fifty-five. Maybe Krampus figured kids are too much trouble and started with us instead."

A ripple of nervous laughter spread through the room, but it didn't quite reach everyone. Rosie leaned forward, her grin sharp. "Well, if that's the case, Gertie, you'd better pack your bags. You're next on his list."

Gertie smirked, tapping her fingers thoughtfully on the table. "If it's not Krampus—and I still say it could be—then we're dealin' with somethin' just as old and mean. And I don't like old and mean."

"Bless your heart, Gertie," Rosie quipped. "That makes two of you, then."

The laughter this time was uneasy, like a tremor rippling through the room.

In the corner, Micky Vermooch sat with Sheriff Emmett, his sharp blue eyes scanning the room, but his mind was elsewhere. His fingers tapped an absent rhythm on the edge of his coffee cup. The description of the man at the meeting clawed at him like a memory he'd tried to bury.

The footage came rushing back—Izzy, the Marsh, and that shadowy figure. Micky had set up the cameras himself, hoping to capture whatever haunted her. After she vanished, the tape revealed a tall, cloaked figure moving with deliberate menace, as if it belonged in the Marsh. Seeing it was like staring into the eyes of something ancient and unyielding.

Now, sitting here, hearing Patricia's description of the man and his coat, Micky felt that same cold hand tighten its grip around his thoughts. That figure wasn't just a memory anymore. It was here, and it wasn't done.

"Micky, you with us?" Emmett's deep voice cut through the haze.

Micky blinked, forcing a tight smile. "Sorry, mate. Drifted off for a moment."

"You've been quieter than usual tonight," Emmett said, his tone probing. "That man got you spooked?"

Micky swirled his coffee, watching the ripples as he spoke. "It's nothing worth mentioning, Sheriff. Just the season playing tricks on an old mind."

Before Emmett could press further, faint footsteps crunched outside, carried by the wind. The sound was gone as quickly as it came, leaving the room eerily silent for a moment. Micky's gaze flicked to the frosted window. For a fleeting second, he thought he saw a shadow slip past, but it was too quick to be sure.

"You see something?" Emmett asked, his voice low.

"Probably just the wind," Micky said, though his gut told him otherwise.

The door burst open then, a gust of icy wind scattering napkins and drawing startled gasps. Cindy Blevins stepped inside, her breath clouding the air, her eyes wide with panic. She clutched something in her hand, her knuckles white.

"Y'all," she began, her voice trembling. "You need to see this."

The room fell silent as she crossed to Micky and Emmett's table. She unwrapped the object in her hands—a key, rusted and jagged, its surface pitted with age.

"This was on my porch," Cindy whispered. "I heard footsteps and thought it was the wind. When I opened the door, this was sitting there."

Tanya leaned forward, her brow furrowed. "That ain't no house key. Looks like something out of a fairy tale—or a nightmare."

Gertie jabbed a finger toward the key. "See? I told y'all! It's Krampus. He's leavin' warnin's."

"Oh, for heaven's sake, Gertie," Rosie snapped. "If it's Krampus, why's he usin' keys? He unlockin' the naughty list now?"

The laughter was brittle, the tension growing thicker.

Micky cleared his throat, his voice calm but commanding. "Keys are often symbolic, love. They open what's been locked away—or remind us of something we've tried to forget."

Gertie narrowed her eyes at him. "You've got a way of makin' things sound real spooky, Micky. Almost like you know somethin' we don't."

Before Micky could respond, Emmett leaned in, his voice a quiet command. "If you've got that footage, I want to see it."

Micky's jaw tightened. He nodded, though his thoughts churned. That tape wasn't meant for anyone else's eyes, but now, it seemed he had no choice.

As Cindy gathered the key and promised to call Emmett if anything else appeared, Micky stepped outside. The cold bit at his skin, but he welcomed the clarity it brought.

Behind him, Gertie stepped closer, her breath visible in the frigid air. "So, what do you think? Supernatural or just our imaginations runnin' wild?"

Micky glanced at her, a faint smile touching his lips. "Supernatural or not, Gertie, it's here. And it's not leaving until it's got what it came for."

In the distance, the wind carried a sound—low, mournful, and hollow. It wasn't the wind. Micky knew that much.

~ 26 ~

THE KEY TO THE MARSH

The cozy warmth of *Bayou Bliss Coffee House* wrapped itself around the morning, offering a comforting haven from the rare Louisiana snow blanketing the streets of Bayou Vista. Outside, the muffled crunch of boots and scrape of tires blended with the stillness of the snow-covered town. Inside, the aroma of chicory coffee and the sweetness of Brenda Menifee's fresh beignets created an inviting sanctuary.

Behind the counter, Brenda adjusted the red and black Christmas garlands draped over the frosted windows. Twinkling lights reflected off the glass, casting a warm glow that flickered like a firelight. She glanced at Cindy Blevins, who sat by the window, her gaze fixed on a rusted key resting on a napkin in front of her.

The key caught the faint morning light, its jagged edges gleaming as if it held a secret waiting to be unearthed. Cindy's hands cradled her coffee mug, though the drink had long since gone cold.

"Still stuck on that ol' thing, huh?" Brenda teased, leaning over the counter. "You've been staring at it so hard I'm surprised it ain't sprouted legs and walked off."

Cindy looked up, her expression troubled. "I can't stop thinking about it, Brenda. Why me? What could this key possibly have to do with me?"

Brenda wiped her hands on her apron and shrugged. "Honey, if I knew the answer, I'd be writing mystery novels instead of slinging coffee."

The bell above the door jingled, letting in a gust of cold air as Patricia and Shannon shuffled inside, their laughter warming the room. Patricia, bundled in scarves, looked like a walking pile of laundry. "Lord Almighty," she exclaimed, stomping snow off her boots. "It's colder than a gator's behind out there!"

Shannon followed, tugging off her gloves. "If this keeps up, we're gonna have to start building igloos."

Brenda chuckled, grabbing the coffee pot. "Well, come on in and thaw out. Coffee's hot, and the beignets are fresh. Don't say I never take care of y'all."

Patricia peeled off her coat, plopping into the seat across from Cindy, while Shannon slid into the chair beside her. Patricia glanced down at the key, her eyes narrowing. "That the one from last night?"

Cindy nodded. "Sure is. I still don't know what to make of it."

Patricia leaned forward. "Did you have any dreams about it?"

Cindy hesitated, her fingers tightening on her mug. "Yeah. There was a cabin—old, falling apart in the Marsh. I could hear a girl crying, calling my name. I tried to get to her, but there was this door, and the key fit it. Then... I woke up."

The table grew quiet, the weight of Cindy's words pressing down like the snow outside. Brenda refilled their mugs, her brow furrowed. "A cabin in the Marsh, huh? That sounds like the Carr place. Ain't nobody been out there in years."

Shannon shivered. "Mama always said the Marsh don't let go of what it takes. The Carrs... they just disappeared one night, supper still sitting on the table."

"You think this key could belong to them?" Cindy asked.

"Could be," Patricia said. "Bayou Vista's got a way of holding on to its ghosts."

The door jingled again as Taylor strolled in, brushing snow off her boots. "Morning, y'all," she said, unwrapping her scarf. "Feels like I'm living in one of those Hallmark movies—except instead of falling in love, I'm freezing to death."

Brenda smirked. "Well, Taylor, if you're waiting on a handsome stranger to sweep you off your feet, you're going to be waiting a while in this town. Now sit down and help Cindy figure out what the devil she's dragged into this café."

Taylor slid into a chair, studying the key. "Where'd you get it?"

"Left on my porch last night," Cindy replied.

Taylor whistled. "If it were me, I'd be changing all my locks."

Brenda chuckled. "That's the difference between you and Cindy—she sees trouble and invites it in for coffee."

The group laughed, but the sound faded as the door jingled again, and Micky Vermooch stepped inside.

Micky's sharp blue eyes swept the room, landing on the group. He nodded politely and made his way over, brushing snow from his long coat.

"Ladies," he greeted, his English accent smooth as silk. "Thought I'd find you here."

Brenda smirked. "Micky, you're like a Sherlock Holmes—only better dressed and easier on the eyes."

Micky smiled faintly, but his gaze dropped to the key. He picked it up, turning it over in his hands. His expression darkened. "Keys unlock more than doors," he said quietly. "Sometimes, they open things best left alone."

Cindy's chest tightened, her hands gripping her mug. She couldn't shake the feeling that Micky wasn't just talking about the Carrs. "What do you mean?"

Micky's eyes flicked to hers, unreadable. "Just that doors don't always lead where you think they will."

Before Cindy could respond, the door opened again, and Sheriff Emmett stepped inside, his heavy boots thudding against the floor. "Morning," he greeted, his tone firm. "So, what's got everybody talking about?"

Cindy nodded, clutching her coffee mug tighter. "Sheriff, do you know where the Carrs' old cabin is?"

Emmett frowned, his expression guarded. "I do, but why are you asking? That place has been abandoned for years. Nothing good ever came out of poking around there."

Cindy leaned forward, her voice steady despite her nerves. "I think this key belongs to that cabin. It feels... connected to me somehow. I need to go out there."

Micky nodded, his expression thoughtful. "She's right, Sheriff. Keys don't just find their way to people without reason. If the Marsh wants her to see something, it'll find a way."

Emmett let out a long sigh, his brow furrowing. "That place is dangerous. The Marsh ain't kind to visitors, especially not ones digging up its secrets."

"I'm not digging," Cindy said firmly. "I'm just... following what feels like a trail."

Emmett adjusted his hat, his tone final. "If we're doing this, we're doing it now. Snow's only going to get worse."

Cindy stood, her nerves warring with determination. She pocketed the key and glanced at Micky and Emmett. "Let's go."

As they stepped out into the icy morning, Brenda called after them, her voice half-joking but laced with genuine worry. "Y'all better come back in one piece, or I'll be the one haunting that Marsh!"

The Marsh grew colder the deeper they went, the air heavy with an unnatural stillness. A sharp crack echoed through the silence as a branch, heavy with snow, snapped and fell to the ground. Cindy jumped, clutching the key tighter, her breath fogging in the icy air.

"You all right?" Micky asked, his tone calm but watchful.

Cindy nodded quickly. "Yeah. Just... I don't know. It feels like the Marsh is watching."

Emmett glanced back at her. "That's because it is."

Finally, they reached the clearing.

The cabin stood like a forgotten relic, its sagging roof heavy with snow. Cindy's breath caught as she stepped forward.

"This is it," she whispered.

Micky touched her arm lightly. "You're not alone, love."

The key slid into the lock, turning with a metallic click. The door groaned open, revealing a dark, musty interior.

Inside, Cindy's eyes landed on a photograph sitting on a dusty table. She picked it up carefully, her heart racing as she studied the faces.

The Carr family smiled back at her—a man, a woman, and a young girl standing outside the cabin. Her gaze froze on the woman.

"That's..." Cindy's voice trailed off, her hands trembling. "That looks like my Aunt Ellen, my mom's sister."

Micky's brow furrowed. "Your mother's sister?"

Cindy nodded, her voice barely a whisper. "She disappeared before I was born. Mama never knew what happened to her."

Micky exchanged a grim look with Emmett. "Looks like you've found your answer, love. But I'm not sure it's one you'll like."

Beneath the table, Cindy noticed a trapdoor. She knelt, pulling it open to reveal a small chest. The lock clicked open, and inside was a stack of yellowed papers.

Micky read aloud:

To whoever finds this—The Marsh does not forget. It does not forgive. What it takes, it keeps. If you're reading this, leave Bayou Vista. The Marsh remembers.

"What does that mean?" Cindy asked, her voice cracking.

"It's a warning," Micky said gravely. "Whatever happened to the Carrs—and Mary Ellen—it's not finished."

That night, Hank Mullins sat alone in his living room, a football game blaring on the TV. Outside, the snow fell softly, blanketing the town in an unnatural stillness.

Then came the knock.

It was sharp and deliberate, breaking through the noise. Hank froze, his breath catching. Slowly, he approached the door, his pulse pounding in his ears.

He opened it cautiously, peering into the cold night. No one was there.

On the porch was a package, neatly wrapped in brown paper and tied with twine.

Hank hesitated, his breath fogging in the air. Something about the package felt wrong, heavy, though it barely weighed anything.

He carried it inside, his hands trembling as he untied the twine. Inside, nestled in a fold of faded cloth, was a cameo pin—the very one Gertie had described. His stomach twisted as he turned it over, his breath hitching at the name engraved on the back: *LaBlanc.*

A memory surfaced, unbidden, sharp and cold as the winter air. His mother, Sarah, had whispered it to him late one night, her voice shaking with a fear he didn't fully understand at the time.

"Your daddy... he's not like other men, Hank," she had said, her eyes darting to the shadows as if she expected him to appear. "He's the clown killer—the one from Devil's Marsh. Billy LaBlanc is your father, and you can't ever let anyone know. Promise me, Hank. Swear it."

Hank had been just a boy then, too young to grasp the full weight of her words, but the fear in her eyes had been unforgettable. He'd nodded, swallowing hard, and vowed to keep her secret. For years, he buried it deep, pretending it had been a bad dream or a twisted story his mother had invented to scare him into silence. But now, holding the pin, the past felt as vivid and undeniable as the cold biting at his skin.

He staggered back from the table, the cameo clutched tightly in his hand. His mother's voice echoed in his mind: *"You can't ever let anyone know."* But someone knew. Whoever left this package on his porch wasn't just reminding him of the secret—this was a warning.

Hank's chest heaved as the realization settled in. He wasn't just tied to the Marsh through blood; he was tethered to its darkness. The kind of darkness that didn't let go.

He turned sharply to the window, his breath fogging the glass as he peered into the snowy night. The stillness of the town felt suffocating, the silence too deliberate. Whoever had left the package could still be out there, watching.

His fingers tightened around the pin, his knuckles white. His mother's warnings weren't enough to prepare him for this. The cameo wasn't just a symbol of his father—it was a threat. Billy LaBlanc's shadow loomed larger than ever, and Hank knew that the Marsh hadn't forgotten.

And now, it seemed, it had come for him.

~ 27 ~

THE INVITATION

The golden morning light spilled through the frosted windows of *Bayou Bliss Coffee House,* softening the festive garlands Brenda Menifee had hung with care. The smell of chicory coffee, sugar-dusted beignets, and a hint of cinnamon floated through the air, promising a warm reprieve from the unusual Louisiana chill gripping Bayou Vista. The snow outside had muffled the usual small-town buzz, but inside, the coffee shop was alive with conversation.

Rosie sat at the corner table, her bright red cardigan offset by the snowflake earrings that dangled as she animatedly recounted her latest story. Across from her, Gertie, wrapped in her quilted winter coat like she was braving the Arctic, sipped her coffee with exaggerated slowness.

"Rosie, honey, if you keep talkin' that loud, the folks over in Cypress Cove are gonna hear you," Gertie teased, her grin sharp as ever.

Rosie rolled her eyes. "Oh, hush, Gertie. Ain't nobody listenin' to me but you, and you're lucky for it. My stories are worth their weight in gold."

Gertie snorted. "Gold? More like fool's gold."

At the counter, Brenda chuckled as she poured fresh coffee. "Y'all play nice, or I'll start charging you by the word."

Shannon, seated near the window, nudged Patricia. "Ain't it something? Only in Bayou Vista do people argue over who's the loudest at eight in the morning."

Patricia smirked, adjusting her scarf. "Well, Shannon, if you're looking for peace and quiet, you've come to the wrong place."

The bell above the door jingled violently, and Hank stormed in, his boots leaving wet tracks on the wooden floor. The sudden gust of cold air silenced the room. Hank's face was as red as the plaid jacket he wore, his jaw set tight and his eyes blazing. He looked like a man ready for a fight.

Behind the counter, Brenda stiffened. "Morning, Hank. Coffee?"

Hank ignored her, his gaze sweeping the room until it landed on Sheriff Johnson, who was nursing his usual black coffee in a corner booth. Without so much as a hello, Hank marched over, his boots pounding like a drumbeat.

"Sheriff," Hank barked, his voice loud enough to rattle the mugs on the counter. "I got somethin' to say."

Emmett raised an eyebrow, his face calm but watchful. "Morning to you too, Hank. What's got you riled up?"

Hank slammed a hand on the table, making the sugar packets jump. "Don't you play dumb with me, Emmett. Someone's stickin' their nose where it don't belong, and I don't think it's funny. Not one damn bit."

The room, already quiet, seemed to hold its breath. Brenda glanced nervously at Micky Vermooch, who had been silently sipping his coffee at the end of the counter. Micky's sharp blue eyes flicked to Hank, his expression unreadable.

"Slow down, Hank," Emmett said evenly, leaning back in his chair. "What are you talking about?"

Hank glared at him, his hands balled into fists. "That's none of your damn business. But I'll tell you this—it stops now. I don't know who's behind it, but they'd best think twice before pokin' the bear."

From her corner, Rosie leaned over to Gertie, whispering loudly enough for half the room to hear, "Sounds like ol' Hank's got a bee in his bonnet."

Gertie snorted. "More like a whole hive."

Hank shot them a look, his glare hard enough to cut glass. "Y'all got somethin' to say?"

"Not a thing," Gertie replied, her smile sweet as sugar. "We're just here for the coffee."

"Enough," Emmett said, his tone firm. He stood, his tall frame towering over Hank. "If you've got a problem, Hank, you need to tell me what's going on. I can't help you if you don't talk."

"I don't need your help," Hank snapped. His voice wavered slightly, a hint of something beneath his anger—fear, maybe. "I need folks to mind their own damn business." He turned on his heel and stormed out, the bell above the door jingling in his wake. He glanced nervously at the small package tucked under his jacket, the memory of the cameo pin and his mother's terrified voice refusing to leave him. "He's not real," he muttered to himself. "Billy's dead. Ain't no damn ghost comin' for me."

"Well," Rosie said, breaking the silence, "if that don't beat all. What crawled up his britches?"

"I reckon we don't wanna know," Shannon murmured, shaking her head.

Micky set his cup down with a soft clink and stood, brushing nonexistent crumbs from his coat. "He's scared," Micky said, his voice low but carrying. "Whatever's bothering him, it's got him good and proper."

Taylor, seated near the counter, frowned. "You think it's about those gifts?"

Before anyone could answer, the door jingled again, and Judge Hopper walked in. His usual jovial demeanor was replaced with a stern, almost haunted expression. He headed straight for the counter, holding a piece of creamy stationery in his hand. Brenda, already holding the coffee pot, poured him a fresh cup without waiting for him to ask.

"Sheriff, I was looking for you," he said, his voice low.

"Join the club," Brenda replied, nodding toward Emmett.

Hopper approached the Sheriff, handing him the note. Emmett read it quickly, his frown deepening.

"Gathering everyone tomorrow night at the Christmas tree?" Emmett said, glancing up. "What's this about?"

Hopper shook his head. "I don't know, but it doesn't feel like a prank."

Micky stepped forward, his voice measured. "This isn't about the Marsh at all, Sheriff. It's about Mary Ellen, the Carr family, and the secrets this town's been burying for generations. She's coming back, and this time, she's not leaving without answers."

The room fell silent again, the weight of his words settling over the group like a heavy quilt. Rosie was the first to break the tension.

"Well, if I'm gonna face some ghostly nonsense, I'm gonna need another cup of coffee," she said, sliding her mug toward Brenda. "Might as well be caffeinated for the apocalypse."

Gertie chuckled, nudging her. "If it's the end of the world, Rosie, I hope you're the first to go. At least then I'll get some peace and quiet."

Micky's lips twitched into a faint smile. "Ladies, if the world ends, I promise I'll save you a spot in the hereafter."

As the conversations picked up again, Brenda refilled cups, her mind racing. Outside, the snow continued to fall, a rare and eerie backdrop for the growing unease in Bayou Vista.

The door jingled again, and in walked Gail, her cheeks flushed from the cold. She paused, taking in the tense atmosphere, before making her way to the counter.

"Morning, Brenda," she said, unwinding her scarf. "Looks like I missed a scene."

"You did," Brenda replied, pouring her a steaming cup of coffee. "Hank was in here, raising Cain about something but wouldn't say what."

Gail raised an eyebrow. "Well, ain't that par for the course with him. Did he at least pay for his coffee?"

"He didn't stop long enough to drink any," Rosie interjected. "Too busy being mad at the world."

Gail chuckled as she took her cup. "Bless his heart. That man's been mad since '85."

Brenda leaned closer, lowering her voice. "Judge Hopper's got a letter too. Says everyone who got one of those gifts is supposed to meet at the Christmas tree tomorrow night."

Gail's expression darkened. "This just keeps getting stranger."

"It sure does," Brenda agreed.

At a corner table, Loretta Cobb sat quietly, her hands wrapped around a mug of hot chocolate. She had been listening intently to the conversations around her, her mind racing. Loretta wasn't one for superstitions, but the air in Bayou Vista had shifted, and it felt heavy, like a storm brewing.

"Taylor," Loretta called softly. "You ever seen anything like this?"

Taylor, who had just sat down with Shannon and Patricia, shook her head. "Not like this. Snow's one thing, but this whole business with the gifts? It's downright eerie."

Shannon leaned forward, her voice low. "Y'all think it's really her? The girl from Preacher's Pond?"

Patricia crossed her arms. "I don't know what I think. But if it is, I can't blame her for stirring up trouble. People around here got a lot to answer for."

Micky approached their table, his boots clicking softly on the wooden floor. "That they do," he said, his accent cutting through the din. "But it's not just about what you did, you see. It's about what you didn't do."

The group fell silent, watching as Micky pulled out a chair and sat down. He folded his hands on the table, his sharp eyes scanning their faces.

"Guilt," he said quietly, "has a funny way of manifesting. Sometimes, it sits quiet, buried deep. Other times, it rises like smoke, impossible to ignore. And I'd wager this town's been smoking for a long time."

Patricia frowned. "What are you saying, Micky? That we are all guilty?"

"Not all," he replied, tilting his head. "But enough."

Rosie, overhearing the conversation, piped up. "Well, I don't know about y'all, but I sleep just fine at night. Whatever this Watcher's lookin' for, it ain't me."

Gertie smirked. "That's because you don't have a conscience, Rosie."

Rosie gasped dramatically, clutching her chest. "How dare you, Gertie! I'll have you know my conscience is just fine. It's my patience that's worn thin."

The room erupted in laughter, a brief reprieve from the tension. Even Micky cracked a smile.

As the day faded into evening, the snow showed no sign of stopping. Brenda lit candles on each table, their flickering flames casting a warm glow over the room. Outside, the town square was quiet, the Christmas tree standing tall and proud in the center, its lights twinkling against the darkening sky.

Inside *Bayou Bliss*, the conversation had shifted to the gathering set for tomorrow night.

"You think everyone will show?" Brenda asked, her voice quiet.

Micky didn't turn from the window, his gaze fixed on the falling snow. "Not everyone," he said finally. "But enough."

"And what happens to the ones who don't?" she pressed.

Micky glanced back at her, his expression unreadable. "They'll wish they had."

~ 28 ~

THE GATHERING

The snowstorm had grown fierce, a swirling wall of white that muffled the familiar sounds of Bayou Vista. Christmas Eve in this Louisiana town hadn't seen weather like this in thirty years. The heavy silence of the square deepened the unease among the gathered crowd.

The Christmas tree stood at the center, its simple lights flickering weakly against the storm. Normally a symbol of warmth and joy, tonight it felt like something else entirely—an unspoken promise, a warning, or perhaps an offering.

Brenda worked briskly at a folding table near the square's edge, handing out steaming cups of chicory coffee. Her gloved hands shook as she poured, spilling a little onto the snow. "Here you go, sugar," she said, passing a cup to Matilda, the school bus driver.

Matilda clutched the tarnished locket in one hand, the coffee in the other. "I shouldn't have come out here, Brenda," she murmured, her voice trembling. "This doesn't feel right. Not one bit."

"Well, none of this feels right," Brenda replied, glancing toward the tree.

A few feet away, Melissa and Tanya stood near Jason, the owner of *Jason's Bar*. She adjusted her scarf against the biting wind, her voice barely audible. "Clara Mae went missing decades ago, and nobody cared. Why is it a problem now?"

Jason shook his head. "We're about to find out."

Cindy stood with her husband, Dondi, owners of *C&D Kwik Stop*. She kept her arms crossed tightly, her eyes darting around the square. "I didn't know Mary Ellen," she muttered. "But I knew Clara Mae and Emily. We all did. And we still didn't say a damn thing when they disappeared."

Dondi nodded grimly. "We all ignored it, Cindy. We thought it was someone else's problem. Now it's ours."

Nearby, Margie stood with her brother Eddie. She leaned in close, her voice low. "You shouldn't have come out here, Eddie. This isn't your fight."

Eddie scoffed. "If it's your fight, Margie, it's mine too. Do you think the Carr family's secrets didn't affect me growing up? We're all tied to this."

Gertie huddled with Rosie and Firecracker near Brenda's coffee stand. Firecracker held her rusted belt buckle tightly, her knuckles white beneath her gloves. "I don't like this," Firecracker whispered. "Why's she coming now, after all these years?"

Gertie snorted. "Because we buried her story with her. Just like we did with Nancy, Joe, Helen, and Donna Lou.

Don't tell me she's not here to hurt us. Bullshit. She's here to make us pay."

Rosie shot Gertie a look. "Keep your voice down. You're gonna rile people up."

Gertie jabbed her coffee cup toward the tree. "Let 'em be scared. Maybe it's what we all need."

Loretta stood between Trisha and Jill, her hands shoved deep into the pockets of her coat as she tried to keep the cold from biting at her fingers. "Do you think she's really here?" Loretta asked, her voice barely above a whisper.

Trisha shrugged, her gaze fixed on the faint glow near the Christmas tree. "I don't know, but this whole thing feels wrong. Like we're standing in a story we don't want to be part of."

Jill hugged herself tightly, her breath fogging in the cold air. "It's not just wrong," she said softly. "It's terrifying. What if this isn't just about our families? What if it's about us too?"

Loretta swallowed hard, her eyes darting between her friends and the crowd. "If it is, I hope she's not looking at me."

Sheriff Emmett stood near the tree with Mayor Steve, adjusting his wide-brimmed hat as snow piled on its brim. His hand brushed the photograph tucked in his pocket, the edges worn from his nervous grip. Spotting Micky Vermooch striding through the storm, Emmett called out, "Micky! Is this it? Is she really coming?"

Micky stopped beside him, brushing snow off his coat. His sharp blue eyes scanned the crowd. "She's already here, Sheriff. You feel it, don't you?"

"What does she want?" Emmett asked.

"The truth," Micky said simply. "And if she doesn't get it, she'll take it."

Across the square, Taylor clutched the tiny baby shoe she'd been left with. "I don't even know how this ties back to me," she said, her voice breaking. "My family didn't know Mary Ellen or the Carrs."

"You sure about that?" Lena, cradling the broken doll she'd received, asked. "Maybe they knew more than they ever said."

Shannon, from *Shanster Travels*, wrung her hands. "I don't understand why I'm here. I didn't know any of them."

Preacher John, standing beside her, murmured, "It's not about what you knew. It's about what you didn't do. Sometimes not helping is worse than hurting."

Shannon's shoulders slumped. "There was a family once that needed help really badly. I didn't have time. I told myself someone else would step in. Guess no one did."

LaDonna whispered to Stephanie, who stood nearby with Tina and Mary from *Bayou Belle Beauty*.

"I'm scared," she admitted, her voice barely audible.

"Me too," Stephanie replied softly, her eyes fixed on the swirling snow.

Gail, Patricia, Catrina, and Cindy Blevins huddled close near the edge of the square, their breaths visible in the icy air as they tried to keep warm.

Gail tightened her coat around her and muttered, "I can't believe we're all out here for this."

Patricia nodded, her eyes darting toward the Christmas tree. "Feels like we've stepped into one of those ghost stories my grandma used to tell. Only this one ain't got a happy ending."

Hank paced near the edge of the crowd, his cameo pin burning cold in his pocket. His face was pale, his breath fogging in the frigid air. "This is insane!" he shouted suddenly, drawing every eye. "She's not real! She can't be real!"

Margie grabbed his arm. "Hank, calm down. You're going to make things worse."

Hank jerked away. "Worse? She's coming for blood, Margie, and you all know it!"

Micky stepped forward, his voice calm but firm. "She's not here for blood, Hank. She's here for the truth."

Hank pointed a trembling finger at Micky. "You don't know that! You think you can talk your way out of this with your fancy English words, but you don't know her."

"She's not a devil," Micky replied evenly. "She's a reckoning."

The church bells rang out, their deep tones reverberating through the square. The crowd fell silent as the snow thickened, the wind carrying a strange stillness. Every breath hung visible in the air.

"She's here," Lena whispered, her voice trembling.

At first, it was just a faint glow in the distance, barely visible through the storm. The light grew brighter, and a figure emerged—cloaked and hooded, moving with deliberate steps. She held a lantern in one hand, its golden light casting an eerie glow.

The lantern swayed, its light touching each of the townsfolk. Brenda clutched her coat tightly. "Micky, what does she want?"

"To remember," Micky said, his voice steady. "And to make you remember."

"I'm scared, Micky," Brenda whispered, her voice trembling. "What if I don't know what to say?"

"Don't worry," Micky said softly, his tone calm and steady. "When the light from the lantern touches you, so will the truth."

The snow swirled unnaturally around her feet, and the light from her lantern seemed to pull the air from the square. People struggled to breathe, their fear as tangible as the cold.

The Watcher's presence felt like a weight pressing down on them all. The lantern's glow seemed to search their faces, pausing briefly on Hank, then on Gertie.

"She's looking at me," Hank whispered, his voice barely audible. His lips trembled as he took a step back.

The Watcher's lantern paused, its golden light falling on Gertie. Her breath hitched as the glow seemed to press on her, making her take an involuntary step forward. Her face hardened, defiance flashing in her eyes. "She can look all she wants," Gertie muttered. "I've got nothing to say."

"You sure about that, Gertie?" Rosie asked quietly, her eyes darting nervously.

"I'm sure," Gertie snapped, though her voice faltered slightly. Her hands trembled as she gripped her coffee cup.

The Watcher raised her free hand, palm outward. The lantern swayed, its glow brightening as if reaching for someone. It stopped suddenly, its golden light falling directly on Hank. His lips trembled as he took a step back.

"What happens if we don't give her what she wants?" someone whispered.

The lantern flared, and the storm roared back to life, a sound that carried with it a single word, whispered but unmistakable:

"Remember."

~ 29 ~

THE WATCHER'S ARRIVAL

The snow hit harder, driving down like a wall of white that erased everything outside the town square. The Christmas tree's lights sputtered weakly, their glow doing little to cut through the swirling storm. The crowd stood frozen, not just by the cold but by something heavier. Fear. Dread. The truth clawing its way up through decades of silence.

The Watcher's lantern swung toward Gertie, the golden light spilling over her like a judgment. Her face hardened, and her voice sliced through the brittle quiet. "Get that damn light off me!" she snapped, her Southern drawl sharp and biting. "I didn't get no gift. This ain't got nothin' to do with me!"

Nobody moved. Nobody dared to breathe. It wasn't just the cold biting at their skin—it was something heavier, a suffocating force that pinned them where they stood. The Watcher's presence wrapped around them like unseen hands, gripping their limbs and holding them

190

still. Even the storm seemed to bow to her power, the howling wind fading into an eerie, oppressive silence.

"What's happening?" Brenda whispered, her hands frozen mid-reach for the coffee pot at her stand. "Why can't we move?"

Matilda's voice quivered. "I—I don't know. I feel stuck, like my boots are nailed to the ground. I can't move, Brenda! What's going on?"

Panic rippled through the crowd. People started shouting, their voices rising above the storm.

"I'm stuck too!" Firecracker yelled, clutching the old, weathered scarf wrapped around her neck like it was a lifeline. "What's she doing to us?"

"Calm down!" Sheriff Emmett barked, but his own voice shook. He tried to take a step forward, but his boots wouldn't budge. "Damn it," he muttered under his breath, gripping the old photograph in his hand.

Micky Vermooch, standing at the front, turned his sharp gaze over the crowd. Snow clung to his long coat, and his rich English accent cut through the chaos like a blade. "Listen up, folks," he said, his voice calm but commanding. "I know you're scared, but it's time to face the music. She's not looking for revenge. She's looking for the truth. And she's not letting us leave until she gets it."

"What kind of truth?" Cindy Morrow shouted from where she stood with her husband, Dondi. "I didn't do anything to that girl! None of us did!"

Micky shook his head, his voice softer now. "It's not just about what you did, love. It's about what you didn't do. What you turned a blind eye to. Secrets got weight, and this town's been carrying them for years."

The Watcher's lantern swayed again, its light fixing back on Gertie. She scowled, her shoulders rigid as she stared it down. "I told you, I ain't got nothin' to say!" she spat, though her voice faltered. "You got the wrong woman."

"Are you sure about that, Gertie?" Rosie Fontenot asked quietly, standing nearby with her arms crossed. Her voice carried just enough edge to slice through the storm. "You always had plenty to say about everybody else."

"Shut up, Rosie," Gertie snapped. But the tension in her voice betrayed her. The lantern's glow seemed to press on her like a weight, and she finally broke, her hands trembling as she clutched her coffee cup. "Fine. I heard her cryin' that night. I heard her screamin'. But I was scared, okay? I thought it wasn't my business!"

The light shifted off Gertie, leaving her trembling, and moved to Matilda. She clutched the tarnished locket like it might save her. "I—I don't even know why I got this," she stammered. "I wasn't alive when Mary Ellen disappeared."

Micky tried to step closer but found his feet frozen to the ground. His gaze remained steady on her. "It's not about you, Matilda. It's about your daddy. He knew something, didn't he?"

Tears welled in Matilda's eyes. "He said Emily Carr was trouble. Said her family wasn't right. But he didn't do anything. He heard her crying at night, but he said it wasn't his problem."

The lantern flared, and suddenly an image flickered in the air. Emily Carr, young and fragile, stood in a yard, tears streaking her face. A shadowy figure loomed behind her, shouting words no one could understand. Matilda screamed as the image shifted—the man struck Emily across the face, and the sound of the blow echoed like a gunshot. "Stop!" Matilda cried, sobbing. "I would've helped you if I'd been there! I swear I would've!"

The vision vanished, and Matilda collapsed to her knees. The grip on her legs released, and she scrambled to her feet. "I can move," she whispered in disbelief. "Can I leave?" She looked to the Watcher, who slowly raised her hand and pointed toward the edge of the square. Matilda ran, her sobs trailing behind her.

The lantern's light shifted to Lena, the librarian. She stood frozen, cradling the broken doll in her arms. "This was hers, wasn't it?" she asked softly.

Micky nodded. "It was. But it's not just the doll, Lena. It's what it represents."

Lena wiped her eyes, her voice thick with emotion. "My mama used to talk about Mary Ellen. Said she was cursed. Said her family was bad news. And I...I spread it too. Emily Carr came to me, asking about Mary Ellen, saying she felt some connection. I told her to stop wasting her time. I didn't believe her. And now Emily's gone too."

The lantern flared again, showing an image of Emily in the library, her face desperate as she pleaded for help.

The vision faded, leaving Lena in tears. The grip on her legs vanished, and the Watcher pointed for her to leave. Lena stumbled away, clutching the doll.

One by one, the lantern's light moved over the crowd. Each time it stopped, another truth came out—

Steve, the mayor, cleared his throat, but the usual confidence in his voice was gone, replaced by unease. He stared down at the withered rose in his hand, its brittle petals crumbling at the edges. "What's this supposed to mean?" he asked, his voice rough. "I've done nothing but try to help this town."

Micky's sharp gaze met his. "Maybe you have, mate," he said evenly. "But what about your grandfather? What's his legacy?"

Steve frowned, his brows knitting together as the lines on his face deepened. "He... he was the mayor back in '48. What's that got to do with me?"

The Watcher's lantern swayed, its golden light casting a shimmering image in the snow—a scene from decades ago. The old courthouse came into view, and a young man stood at the podium, speaking to a small crowd. Steve's grandfather. His voice rang out, loud and dismissive. "A family like that ain't worth our trouble. Bayou Vista takes care of its own."

Steve's breath caught, his grip on the rose tightening. "I didn't know," he said, his voice barely above a whisper. "He never told me about this."

"But his words shaped the town, didn't they?" Micky said, his voice steady but laced with quiet intensity. "And whether you like it or not, you carry his name. That's why you're standing here now."

Steve looked down at the fragile rose, his shoulders sagging under the weight of realization. "I'm so sorry," he said, his voice breaking. "I'd never turn my back on someone. Never."

As the words left his lips, the suffocating grip of the Watcher's power lifted from him. Steve stumbled slightly, testing his freedom, and then turned his gaze to the hooded figure. "Can I go?"

The Watcher raised her hand and pointed toward the edge of the square. Without hesitation, Steve clutched the rose to his chest and walked away, the snow swallowing the sound of his footsteps.

Melissa, the schoolteacher, stood frozen, her hands trembling as she clutched the small brass bell like it was the only thing anchoring her. Her voice quivered, breaking the uneasy silence. "This... this has to do with Emily Carr," she said, her eyes glistening. "She came to me for help once. She told me her daddy was hurting her. I was fresh out of college, scared to make a mistake, scared to get involved. I didn't know if she was telling the truth or just trying to get back at him. I—I turned her away."

Her voice cracked, and she looked down at the bell, its cold metal biting into her skin. "I didn't mean to ignore her. I was just afraid. I thought... I thought maybe it wasn't as bad as she said. But what if it was? What if—" Her words dissolved into a shaky breath as tears began to roll down her cheeks.

The Watcher's lantern flared, its golden light spilling across the square. A vision shimmered into focus, pulling the crowd into a haunting moment. Emily appeared, her face pale and streaked with tears as she ran through the marsh. Her mouth opened in a scream, but no sound came, only the faint, eerie chime of a bell ringing through the heavy air. The image faded as Emily disappeared into the swirling darkness of the marsh.

Melissa let out a strangled sob, gripping the bell so tightly it seemed like she might crush it. "I didn't do anything," she whispered, her voice cracking under the weight of her guilt. "I should have helped her. I should've believed her... I didn't know, but that doesn't make it right." She looked up, her face streaked with tears. "I'm so sorry," she choked out, her words carried away on the cold wind. "Emily... I'm so sorry."

The Watcher's lantern dimmed slightly, as if acknowledging her confession. Slowly, the weight that had held Melissa frozen lifted. She staggered back, her breath hitching as she tested her freedom. "Can I... can I go?" she asked, her voice trembling.

The Watcher raised her hand, pointing toward the edge of the square. Melissa hesitated for a moment, clutching the bell close to her chest, before turning and walking away, her sobs blending with the wind as the snow swallowed her steps.

Shannon, from *Shanster Travels*, stood frozen in place, her hands trembling as she held the sand timer. Its faint glow flickered in the Watcher's golden light, casting eerie shadows on her face. Her voice wavered as she spoke, each word heavy with unease. "What's it got to do with Mary Ellen?" she said, her eyes darting toward Micky.

Micky's sharp gaze met hers, his tone calm yet pointed. "Your family owned land near the marsh, didn't they?"

Shannon nodded slowly, her breath fogging in the icy air. "Yeah... my granddaddy sold it to her daddy. He said it wasn't worth anything. Said he didn't care what happened there."

The Watcher's lantern flared, and an image shimmered into focus in the swirling snow. A small, dilapidated shack near the marsh appeared, its windows dark and lifeless. The air around it seemed to pulse with a suffocating heaviness. A man—Shannon's grandfather—stood nearby, his face set in indifference as he shook his head and walked away.

Micky's voice cut through the tense silence. "He knew what was happening in that house," he said, his words laced with quiet intensity. "But he didn't care. He washed his hands of it and turned his back on her."

Shannon's fingers tightened around the sand timer, her knuckles white. Her face paled as the weight of Micky's words settled over her. "And now we're paying for it," she whispered, her voice barely audible. Her eyes glistened with unshed tears. "I would've never turned away. Not if I'd known."

The Watcher's light flickered as if in acknowledgment. Slowly, she raised her hand and pointed toward the edge of the square. Shannon hesitated for a moment, the sand timer trembling in her grasp, before finally stepping away. Her footsteps crunched softly in the snow as she disappeared into the storm, her head bowed in silent regret.

Finally, the light landed on Sheriff Emmett. He stood tall, though his face was pale as he held up the old photograph. "This is from when she went missing," he said. "My granddaddy was sheriff then. He turned her away. He said it wasn't worth his time. And now...I'm paying for it."

The lantern glowed brighter, showing an image of Mary Ellen in the sheriff's office, her eyes wide with fear and desperation. The sheriff waved her off, his face hard and unyielding. The vision faded, and Emmett bowed his head. "I'm sorry," he whispered. "I'm sorry for what he did."

The Watcher's light dimmed, and she pointed for Emmett to leave. He took a deep breath and stepped away, his boots crunching in the snow.

The storm still raged, but something had shifted. Nervous chatter rippled through the crowd, voices hushed and frantic. "What's happening?" someone whispered, their voice trembling. "Why can't we leave?"

One by one, the weight holding them down began to lift—only for those who confessed. They stumbled away, their steps unsteady but free. Yet those who stayed silent remained rooted in place, their faces pale with fear as the Watcher's lantern continued its relentless, probing search.

Micky stood firm, his eyes meeting the Watcher's hooded gaze. "She's not done yet," he said softly. "There's more to come."

The snow swirled around the square, but it wasn't just snow anymore. It carried the weight of memories, the echoes of a story this town had tried too hard to forget. And the Watcher? She wasn't leaving until it was finished.

~ 30 ~

THE WATCHER'S
JUDGEMENT

The snow fell harder now, cascading from the heavens in relentless sheets that blanketed Bayou Vista in an unnatural silence. It was the kind of storm that swallowed sound, turning even the faintest whisper into nothing. The Christmas tree in the town square, adorned with twinkling lights and ornaments, seemed out of place against the suffocating darkness. Its festive glow flickered weakly, as if struggling to keep the storm and the fear at bay.

The crowd stood frozen, unable to move. They weren't held by the cold alone—though it gnawed at their skin and seeped into their bones. No, this stillness was different. It was her.

The Watcher stood in the middle of the square, her hooded figure barely visible beneath the swirling snow. Her lantern swung gently, its golden light slicing through the storm with an eerie precision. It wasn't just light; it was judgment. Every swing of the lantern sent a ripple of tension through the crowd, though none could flinch or recoil. They could only stand and endure.

Brenda Menifee, stuck near her *Bayou Bliss Coffee House* cart, whispered to Cindy Blevins. Her voice was so soft it barely carried above the howl of the wind. "I've never felt anything like this," Brenda murmured, her lips trembling. "It's like the air itself is holding me down. Cindy, what's happening to us?"

Cindy clutched the rusted key she'd been left, her fingers red and raw from gripping it so tightly. Her tears froze as they rolled down her cheeks, but she couldn't wipe them away. Her arms, her legs—everything felt locked in place. "I don't know," she whispered back, her voice shaking. "I... I can't feel my legs. I can't even move my hands right."

"It's not the storm," Brenda remarked, her voice quivering.

"It's her," Cindy said, her voice cracking. "She's the one keeping us here."

Dondi, standing rigid beside Cindy, let out a low growl of frustration. His face was pale, his breath coming in visible puffs. "What's she waiting for?" he muttered, his voice tight with fear. "Why doesn't she just do whatever she came here to do and let us go?"

"Amen," his wife remarked.

Across the square, Tanya from *Tanya's Crawfish Shack* whimpered softly, her lips trembling as she whispered, "No storm like this ever hit Bayou Vista."

"It's not real," LaDonna hissed through clenched teeth. Her breath hitched as she glanced toward the Watcher. "This... this is her doing. This is some kind of curse."

The crowd held their collective breath as the Watcher's lantern swung again. Its golden light moved slowly, deliberately, sweeping across the gathered towns-folk like a hunter searching for prey. Every second it took felt like an eternity. The tension grew thicker with each pass, pressing down on their chests until it was hard to breathe.

When the lantern stopped on Taylor from *Taylor Trea-sures*, a collective gasp rippled through the crowd. Taylor let out a choked sob, clutching the tiny baby shoe in her trembling hands. Her breath came in short, shallow gasps, her chest heaving against the invisible force hold-ing her in place.

"This was my grandmama's," Taylor said, staring into the light as if searching for answers. Her voice shook so badly it was almost unintelligible. "She kept it in a box under her bed. She said it belonged to a baby that didn't make it. But... but that ain't true."

Micky, standing frozen just beyond the reach of the crowd. Snow clung to the folds of his long coat, and his sharp blue eyes glinted in the lantern's glow. His calm, steady presence was a stark contrast to the fear radiating from everyone else. He spoke softly, his English accent lending an otherworldly quality to his words.

"That's it, Taylor. Just look into the light, and what she wants will come to you," he said, his voice soft and coaxing. He tilted his head slightly. "It wasn't just any baby, was it, love?"

Taylor shook her head, tears freezing on her cheeks. "No. It was Clara Mae's," she admitted, her voice breaking. "My granddaddy found it in the marsh one night. He... he never told nobody. Just brought it home and hid it away."

The lantern flared, and an image shimmered in the snow. A man knelt by the edge of the marsh, his face grim as he picked up the tiny shoe and slipped it into his pocket. The image lingered for a moment, then faded, leaving Taylor shaking.

"Why didn't he say something?" Taylor cried, her voice raw with emotion. "Why didn't he tell someone?"

"Because he didn't want to get involved," Micky said gently, his gaze steady. "But the truth doesn't disappear, love. It waits. And now it's waiting for you to make it right."

Taylor's sobs echoed faintly against the storm as she clutched the shoe tighter. "I'm sorry," she whispered. "I'm so sorry for what he did."

The lantern dimmed slightly, and the air around Taylor seemed to release. She let out a shuddering breath, stumbled backward, and then bolted. Her sobs trailed off as she disappeared into the swirling snow.

The lantern moved again.

When it stopped in front of Tina from *Bayou Belle Beauty,* the crowd seemed to tense as one. Tina's lips quivered, and her hands shook so violently the small music box in her grasp almost fell. The faint melody that drifted out was haunting, its sweet tune almost mocking the terror that filled the square.

"This was hers," Tina said, her voice barely audible. "Mary Ellen's daddy sold it to my granddaddy for a few dollars. Said he needed the money."

"And your family knew, didn't they?" Micky asked, his voice low but pointed.

Tina nodded, her tears freezing on her cheeks. "Mama told me everyone knew what was happening in that house, but they said it wasn't our place to interfere. Said it was better to mind our own business."

The lantern flared again, and another image appeared in the snow. Mary Ellen sat on a rickety porch, clutching the music box to her chest. Her lips moved silently, singing to herself, but her eyes were hollow, empty.

"I'm sorry," Tina sobbed. "I'm so sorry..."

Each confession wrung sobs and gasps from the crowd, their fear growing with each new revelation. Those who confessed were released, their legs freed from the snow's grip, and they fled as fast as they could, vanishing into the storm.

But for those who remained, the weight of the Watcher's presence grew heavier. The air pressed harder against their chests, and the golden light of the lantern burned brighter, sharper.

The golden light moved again, settling on Firecracker from *Berry's Market*. Her usual sharp, sassy demeanor was gone, replaced by something raw and vulnerable. In her hands was a battered diary, its cover faded and the pages yellowed and torn. Her lips quivered as she stared at it, her breath hitching in the freezing air.

"This was my aunt's," Firecracker said, her voice quieter than anyone had ever heard it. "She worked for Mary Ellen's family, back when it all happened."

The lantern flared brighter, and the wind around Firecracker seemed to still. Her words tumbled out in a rush, like she couldn't hold them back anymore. "She wrote about the fights, the screams... she said Mary Ellen's daddy was mean. She knew something bad was happening. She wrote it all down."

"Did she show anyone?" Micky asked, his gaze piercing.

Firecracker shook her head, her tears falling freely now. "No. She needed the job too much. She said it wasn't her place to get involved. My mom ripped out the pages and gave the diary to me."

The lantern flared, and a vision appeared in the snow. A shadowy figure loomed over a young Mary Ellen, who sat curled in a corner, her face streaked with tears. The sound of shouting echoed faintly through the vision, growing louder and more violent. The figure raised a hand, and Mary Ellen flinched, covering her head with her arms.

Firecracker let out a strangled sob as the vision shifted. The door to the house opened, and her aunt stood there, clutching a notebook to her chest. Her face was pale, her eyes wide with fear as she listened to the shouting inside. For a moment, she hesitated, her hand reaching for the door. But then she shook her head and turned away, closing the door softly behind her.

"She should've gone in there," Firecracker whispered, her voice breaking. "She should've done something. But she was scared. She was scared of what might happen if she got involved. She needed that job too bad."

Micky's gaze softened, but his tone remained firm. "And now her silence is yours to carry."

Firecracker hugged the diary to her chest, tears streaking down her face. "I'm sorry," she said, her voice cracking. "She should've helped her. She should've done something. And now it's too late."

The lantern's light dimmed, and Firecracker's legs buckled as the grip holding her in place released. She staggered back, clutching the diary—like it was the only thing keeping her upright. Without another word, she turned and ran, her figure disappearing into the storm.

The Watcher's lantern swung again, its golden light piercing through the storm before stopping in front of Stephanie from *Bayou Belle Beauty*. She gasped, her breath hitching as the glow surrounded her. The small, snuffed-out candle trembled in her hands, its cracked wax cold and brittle.

Stephanie's lips parted, but no words came. The air seemed heavier now, pressing down on her chest like a weight she couldn't shake. Her wide eyes flicked toward Micky, who stood frozen near the edge of the square, snow gathering on his shoulders. Though he couldn't move, his calm voice carried through the silence.

"It's about the light, love," Micky said, his English accent cutting cleanly through the tension. His sharp blue eyes locked on hers, steady and unyielding. "It's not just the candle. It's what it stands for. What your family let go out."

Stephanie's hands shook, the candle rattling faintly against the icy wind. "I—I don't know what it means," she stammered, her voice cracking. "I don't understand."

"Look into the light, love," Micky replied, his voice soft but firm. "Your family saw her, didn't they? Mary Ellen, out in the marsh."

Stephanie nodded, tears spilling down her cheeks and freezing there. "My daddy used to tell a story," she whispered. "Said my grandma saw her one night, out in the marsh with a candle. She was crying—just crying and waving the light, like she was calling to someone."

The lantern flared, its golden light brighter now, casting a vision in the snow. Mary Ellen crouched in the marsh, her small hands clutching a flickering candle. Her face was streaked with tears, her lips moving as though she was whispering a desperate plea.

Stephanie let out a strangled sob, her grip tightening on the candle. "Grandma didn't go to her. She said... she said she was scared. Said it wasn't her place to get involved."

The vision shifted, showing Stephanie's grandmother standing on the edge of the marsh. Her face was pale, her hands trembling as she watched Mary Ellen's light falter. The candle in Mary Ellen's hands flickered weakly, the flame struggling against the wind. Stephanie's grandmother turned and walked away, leaving Mary Ellen to the darkness.

"She let her die out there," Stephanie whispered, her voice breaking. "She let her light go out because she was scared. She should've helped her."

The Watcher's light burned brighter, pressing against Stephanie like a living thing. Her knees buckled, and she let out a choked sob. "I'm sorry," she cried. "I'm so sorry..."

The light dimmed slightly, releasing Stephanie from its grip. She staggered, nearly dropping the candle as she struggled to stand. Without a word, she turned and ran, her footsteps swallowed by the storm.

Finally, the light landed on Hank Mullins. His massive frame seemed even larger under the glow of the lantern, but his face was hard, his jaw set. His hands gripped the cameo he'd been left so tightly his knuckles turned white.

"Hank," Micky said softly. "It's your turn, mate."

"I ain't got nothin' to say," Hank growled, his voice low and defiant.

"You do," Micky said. "And you know it."

The lantern's light flared brighter, hotter, pressing against Hank like a physical force. The crowd, still frozen, could only watch in silent terror as the storm seemed to center on him. The air vibrated with tension, the weight of the moment almost unbearable.

"Hank!" Cindy Morrow cried, her voice breaking. "Please, just say it! Please!"

But Hank stayed silent, his shoulders stiff. The light burned brighter, the storm screaming louder as the vortex of snow and wind intensified around him.

"Don't make her take it from you," Micky warned, his voice cutting through the chaos. "If she does, it'll burn worse than hell."

The clock in the square struck midnight, its chime slicing through the storm like a knife. And still, Hank said nothing.

~ 31 ~

THE DENIAL

The snowstorm howled, its icy breath tearing through Bayou Vista like a wild beast on the hunt. The towering Christmas tree in the square, with its twinkling lights and delicate ornaments, seemed pitiful against the raging storm. The lights flickered in desperation, as if trying to fight back the darkness swallowing the square. Snow whirled in relentless spirals, obscuring the edges of the gathering. Yet no one dared to look away from the Watcher.

She stood firm at the heart of it all, her hooded figure barely visible beneath the swirling snow. The golden glow of her lantern sliced through the storm like a blade, its light unyielding and alive. Frozen in place by something far stronger than the cold, the townsfolk could only watch as the lantern swung toward Hank Mullins.

The cameo in Hank's hand seemed to gleam in defiance, its delicate engraving catching the lantern's glow. But his hand trembled, and his usually proud shoulders hunched like he was carrying the weight of Devil's Marsh itself.

"Why's it stopping at Hank?" Patricia whispered, her voice cracking. She stood stiff, her hands clutching her scarf like it might protect her from the storm—or the truth.

Gail glanced nervously at Patricia, her breath visible in the icy air. "What could Hank have to do with this? He doesn't seem the type, does he?"

Rosie, always quick to speak her mind, let out a sharp, disbelieving laugh. "Don't seem the type?" she snapped, her voice rising. "Ain't nobody's hands clean in this town, Gail. You think we all ain't got somethin' to hide? Maybe Hank's just hidin' the worst of it."

LaDonna shifted uncomfortably, her gloved hands twisting together. "The Watcher doesn't stop at you unless there's something to uncover," she said in a hushed voice. "Lord, what if he's been carrying a secret this whole time?"

The crowd stood like frozen statues, their whispers the only movement in the oppressive stillness. Murmurs rippled through them like a wave of nervous energy, low and frantic. The whispers weren't just about Hank anymore—they were about themselves, their neighbors, and the sins they'd buried alongside Mary Ellen.

The lantern flared brighter, its golden light casting long streaks across the snow. The low hum it emitted deepened, growing louder until it vibrated in the very air.

The crowd held their breath as the glow began to take shape, forming an image before their eyes.

A man appeared, standing deep in Devil's Marsh. He wore a wide-brimmed hat that shadowed his face, and in his hand dangled the same cameo now clenched in Hank's fist. The man turned slightly, just enough for his face to become visible. The crowd gasped.

"That's the man who stood at the back of the church during the town meeting," Cindy Blevins gasped.

"That's Billy LaBlanc," Rosie said, her voice cutting through the stunned silence like a whip. "I'd know that bastard anywhere."

Gertie's hand flew to her mouth, her breath hitching. "Billy LaBlanc," she whispered, her voice shaking. "The man who cursed this town just by livin' in it. The devil himself wouldn't want him in hell."

Margie shivered, clutching her coat tighter. "They said he killed his family... dragged them all out to the marsh one night and left them there to rot."

Micky's gaze stayed on Hank, unrelenting. "That was your daddy, wasn't it?" he asked, his voice low but piercing. "Billy LaBlanc, the man who carried his sins into the marsh and buried them beneath the cypress trees."

Tanya from Tanya's Crawfish Shack clutched her coat tighter, her lips trembling as she spoke. "Billy LaBlanc wasn't just a man," she said, her voice shaking. "He was a monster. My granddaddy said he'd come knocking on doors late at night, taking whatever he wanted—money, food, people. Nobody dared cross him."

LaDonna nodded, her face pale. "Mama said he had the devil's own mark. Wherever Billy went, death wasn't far behind. They say the marsh swallowed him because even hell didn't want him."

"Enough of this!" Hank barked suddenly, his voice cutting through the murmurs. His grip on the cameo tightened, and his face was red with anger. "I ain't got nothin' to do with that man! My daddy's name was Samuel Mullins, and that's the truth!"

The lantern flared again, and the image shifted. Billy was at the edge of Preacher's Pond, his hands caked with dirt and his face twisted with rage. He dragged a limp body across the frozen ground—a girl in a tattered dress, her red hair matted with mud and blood.

Loretta let out a strangled sob. "That's Mary Ellen," she whispered, her voice cracking. "Lord, he's carrying her like she doesn't weigh anything at all."

The vision followed Billy as he trudged through the town under the cover of night. The storm raged even then, its howling winds masking the sound of his heavy footsteps. The marsh loomed ahead, its gnarled trees clawing at the sky like skeletal fingers. Billy dug feverishly beneath an ancient cypress, his breath clouding the air as he muttered to himself.

"Ain't nobody gonna know," Billy's voice rasped, low and gravelly, echoing through the square. "This stays between me and the marsh."

Hank staggered back, his chest heaving like he was struggling to draw breath. "That ain't true!" he bellowed, his voice raw. "My daddy wasn't no killer! He wasn't a monster!"

Micky's voice was calm but sharp, cutting through the tension. "The marsh don't lie, mate. And neither does that cameo. You've always known it, haven't you?"

"No!" Hank shouted, his voice cracking under the weight of the accusation. He threw the cameo to the ground, the metal sinking into the snow with a dull thud. "You're all tryin' to pin somethin' on me that ain't mine! My family didn't have nothin' to do with Mary Ellen!"

The crowd erupted into murmurs, their voices frantic and overlapping.

"He knew," Tricia hissed, her eyes narrowing. "He's known all this time, and he never said a damn word!"

Loretta clutched her scarf tighter, her voice trembling. "How many secrets have we buried in this town? Lord, if Billy was his real daddy..."

Jill crossed herself, her voice barely above a whisper. "The marsh don't forget. And it don't forgive."

The lantern's light pulsed again, its golden glow almost alive as it seemed to draw closer to Hank. A new vision unfolded in the swirling snow. A young boy sat on a rickety porch, clutching the same cameo. His face was streaked with tears, and a woman knelt in front of him, her voice shaking with urgency.

"Don't you ever tell anyone, Hank," she said, her eyes wide with fear. "Your real daddy's name don't leave this house. You hear me? It's the only reason we're still breathin'."

The boy nodded slowly, his small hands gripping the cameo—like it was a lifeline.

The crowd fell into a stunned silence, the whispers dying as the weight of the truth settled over them. Gail's voice broke the quiet, trembling with disbelief. "Billy LaBlanc was his daddy... Lord, help us. That means—"

"Shut up!" Hank roared, his face contorted with fury. "You don't know nothin'! None of you do!"

But the lantern's glow intensified, its light pressing down on him like a physical force. The storm around him seemed to tighten, the wind howling louder as the marsh itself appeared to come alive.

The air grew thick with a new sound—whispers. Faint and fragmented, they seemed to come from the storm itself. Names, cries, and accusations swirled around the square like ghostly echoes.

"Billy..." one voice murmured, so soft it was almost swallowed by the wind.

"Murderer..." came another, louder this time.

The crowd stiffened, their eyes darting toward the marsh's edge. The whispers grew louder, more insistent, like the marsh was calling for Hank.

Micky's gaze remained on Hank, his voice low and steady. "The marsh remembers, mate. And it's been waiting for you."

The Watcher stepped closer, her lantern's light growing so bright it burned against the snow. Hank's knees buckled, and for a moment, it looked like he might fall.

But then he straightened, his face hardening with defiance.

"I don't owe her nothin'," he growled, his voice shaking with anger. "Whatever happened back then, it ain't my fault."

The lantern flared one last time. The snow around Hank whipped into a violent vortex, clawing at his clothes and skin like unseen hands. The whispers rose to a deafening roar, the storm's voice a chaotic symphony of the past.

The crowd gasped as Hank's figure began to fade, his body swallowed by the swirling snow. His screams echoed briefly, a desperate cry that was cut off as the storm silenced itself. When the snow settled, nothing remained but the blackened cameo lying on the frozen ground.

The silence that followed was almost unbearable. The crowd stared at the spot where Hank had stood, their faces pale and drawn.

"Where'd he go?" Brenda whispered, her voice trembling.

Micky's sharp blue eyes lingered on the blackened cameo. His expression was grim as he spoke. "The marsh took him," he said quietly. "And it doesn't give back what it claims."

Loretta crossed her arms tightly over her chest, her voice trembling with anger. "If that's what it does to a man with secrets... what's it gonna do to the rest of us?"

The Watcher turned away, her lantern swinging gently as she moved toward the next soul. The storm settled slightly, the wind calming to an eerie stillness. Somewhere in the distance, the clock tower struck midnight, each chime ringing out like a countdown.

The reckoning wasn't over.

~ 32 ~

THE JUDGEMENT

The snow fell softer now, though it still thickened the air, clinging to the edges of the square like a white veil. The once-raging storm had quieted, but the tension remained, hanging heavy over the town of Bayou Vista. The Christmas tree in the middle of the square twinkled faintly, its lights glowing like a faint promise of hope—or a reminder of what they had lost.

The crowd, smaller now, remained frozen in place, huddled together near the tree. Those who had confessed earlier had fled, desperate to escape the Watcher's unrelenting gaze. The ones left behind stood in uneasy silence, their breath misting in the icy air. Eyes darted nervously from one face to another, searching for reassurance that would never come. The square felt emptier, lonelier, and colder with every passing second.

Micky Vermooch stood near the edge of the crowd, snow dusting his dark coat and long hair. His sharp blue eyes scanned the remaining faces, his voice breaking the uneasy quiet. "She's still waiting," he said, his English ac-

218

cent clear and steady. "There's more to be said, and she won't leave until it's done."

The Watcher's lantern swayed gently, the golden light moving like it had a mind of its own. It hovered over the crowd, passing slowly from face to face, searching. The weight of the light seemed to press against everyone, forcing them to stay rooted where they stood, unable to look away.

The lantern stopped in front of Gertie, a small but sturdy woman with a reputation for her sharp tongue and quick temper. Tonight, though, she looked different—smaller somehow, like the years had finally caught up with her. Her lined face was pale, her lips pressed into a thin line.

"I do know what this is about," Gertie said, her voice trembling slightly but firm enough to carry through the square. "I was 6 years old when Mary Ellen vanished. And my family knew what her daddy was doing to her. We all knew."

A murmur rippled through the crowd, uneasy and low. Gertie ignored it, her gaze fixed firmly on the Watcher's lantern. "My mom and dad told themself it wasn't their place," she continued, her voice breaking slightly. "They told me and my sister it wasn't our business. But it was. We should've done somethin'. We should've spoken up. And then one day, she was gone."

Brenda Menifee gasped softly, clutching her scarf tighter around her neck. "Lord have mercy," she whispered, shaking her head. "Everyone knew something was wrong."

Gertie turned to face the crowd now, her voice softer but filled with regret. "I'm sorry," she said. "We should've done more. We should've tried to stop it."

Micky nodded, his face thoughtful. "It's never easy to admit what you didn't do," he said, his voice calm but carrying a weight of understanding. "But you've done it now, love. That's what matters."

The light from the lantern brightened briefly, then shifted away from Gertie. She let out a shaky breath, her shoulders sagging as though a weight had been lifted.

The lantern drifted again, stopping in front of Rosie. The crowd stilled as the light rested on her, brighter now, as if demanding her attention. Rosie, always loud and brash, looked smaller than anyone had ever seen her. Her face was tight with fear, her hands shaking as they clenched and unclenched at her sides.

She hesitated, her breath visible in short, sharp puffs of air. Finally, her voice broke through the silence, low but steady. "I was there," she said, her words almost swallowed by the snow. "The night she disappeared. I saw her runnin'. I saw her daddy chasin' after her. And I didn't stop him."

The crowd gasped. Tricia, standing near the back, whispered, "Oh my God."

"I was just a kid," Rosie continued, her voice breaking. "I didn't know what to do. But I should've done somethin'. I should've told someone."

The lantern glowed brighter, casting a soft light around Rosie. The snow at her feet cleared slightly, creating a path leading out of the square. Rosie let out a shaky breath, her tears spilling freely now. "I'm sorry," she said, her voice trembling. "I'm so, so sorry."

She turned and began to walk away, her figure disappearing into the falling snow. The crowd watched her leave, their murmurs rising again.

The lantern paused next in front of Mr. Dupree, the oldest man in Bayou Vista. He stood tall despite his age, his face hard and his lips set in a scowl. The golden light reflected off his glasses, but he didn't flinch. Instead, he crossed his arms over his chest, defiant.

"I don't have nothin' to say," Mr. Dupree said flatly, his voice low and gravelly. "Whatever happened to that girl, it wasn't my fault. I didn't have nothin' to do with it."

Micky blue eyes narrowed. "You owned the land by Preacher's Pond, didn't you?" he asked, his voice sharp. "You knew what was happening in that house. You knew her daddy."

The old man's jaw tightened, his eyes narrowing. "I don't owe y'all nothin'," he snapped. "I kept my mouth shut back then, and I'll keep it shut now."

The lantern's light grew brighter, almost blinding. The wind picked up suddenly, howling through the square and whipping the snow into a violent swirl around Mr. Dupree. The crowd gasped, their faces pale with fear.

"Micky," Brenda whispered, clutching his arm. "What's happening?"

"She's taking him," Micky said softly. "The marsh doesn't forget."

The wind roared louder, the snow engulfing Mr. Dupree completely. His cane clattered to the ground, the only thing left behind when the storm settled.

The lantern moved again, stopping briefly in front of others who stood silent and defiant. Each time, the storm grew fiercer, swallowing them one by one. The crowd shrank with each passing moment, the fear thick in the air as people began to realize how many were missing.

Gail glanced around, her voice rising in panic. "Where's Mr. Smith? Has anyone seen Mr. Smith?"

Patricia clutched her coat, her face pale. "He was right here," she whispered. "He was standing right here a second ago."

More voices joined in, frantic and searching. "Mama! Where's Mama?" one young woman called, her voice breaking.

"I can't find my brother!" someone else cried, their voice lost in the storm.

The square became a chaotic mix of sobs and shouts as people realized who was gone. The ones left behind clung to each other, their faces pale and drawn.

The Watcher's lantern dimmed slightly, the golden glow softer now. She turned away from the crowd, her figure retreating toward the edge of the square. The storm calmed further, the snow falling gently again, almost peaceful.

The Christmas tree's lights glowed steadily, their warmth a faint reminder of normalcy in a night that had been anything but.

Micky stood silently as the crowd began to disperse, each person carrying the weight of what they had seen. Some left in groups, clinging to each other for comfort. Others walked alone, their heads bowed against the cold.

Micky stayed behind, his sharp blue eyes fixed on the darkened edge of the square where the Watcher had disappeared. The lantern's glow was gone now, but the tension in the air lingered, heavy and unshakable.

As the snow fell softly around him, Micky's thoughts turned to Hank. The marsh had claimed him, just as it had claimed so many others. But Micky knew the truth. Hank wasn't Billy LaBlanc's only son.

"There's still Micah," Micky murmured to himself, his voice barely audible over the faint hum of the Christmas lights.

The marsh wasn't finished.

~ 33 ~

CHRISTMAS MORNING

The bell at *St. Theresa's Church* tolled deep and steady, its chime rolling through the snow-covered streets of Bayou Vista. The town felt like a snow globe someone had shaken just hours before, leaving behind a serene but haunting stillness. Children weren't running through the streets, no carolers were singing, and the usual Christmas cheer seemed muted under the weight of the night before. Even the stray dogs that often roamed the square seemed to sense the unnatural quiet, their pawprints the only marks on the pristine snow.

The air smelled faintly of woodsmoke from fireplaces, a rare scent for this part of Louisiana, where snow was more legend than reality. The faint sound of someone playing a harmonica drifted from an alley near *Jason's Bar*, the melody soft and mournful before fading into the distance. Every corner of Bayou Vista seemed wrapped in a quiet tension, the kind that lingered after a storm.

The church doors creaked open as folks trickled in, stomping snow from their boots and brushing frost from their coats. Inside, candles flickered along the stained-glass windows, casting a warm glow over the wooden pews. The scent of pine mingled with the faint, musty smell of old hymnals. A Christmas tree near the altar stood tall, adorned with white lights and red ribbons, a beacon of hope in a room filled with solemn faces.

Brenda Menifee sat in the front pew, her usual bright demeanor dimmed. LaDonna squeezed her hand, whispering, "You okay?" Brenda nodded but didn't reply, her gaze fixed on the pulpit. Her other hand clutched a small, fraying Bible, the edges of its pages worn from years of use. The sight of the book brought back memories of her late grandmother, who had always sat in the same spot on Christmas mornings, her voice the loudest during hymns. Brenda could almost hear her now, belting out "O Holy Night" with enough fervor to shake the rafters.

Behind them, Loretta shifted uncomfortably in her seat, glancing back toward the doors every few minutes. Cindy and Dondi Morrow filed in, their heads low, Cindy clutching a thermos of coffee like it was her lifeline. Her red gloves, dusted with snow, trembled slightly as she held it. Dondi whispered something to her, but she only shook her head. He placed a protective hand on her shoulder, glancing around as if daring anyone to question why they were late.

Tanya from the crawfish shack sat near the back, her face pale but set, a thick scarf wrapped tightly around her neck. Jason from the bar leaned in close to Firecracker, whispering something. Firecracker, normally full of sass, simply nodded, her arms crossed tightly over her chest. Her short hair was pulled back, a stark contrast to the elaborate styles she usually sported. Her boots, scuffed and wet, tapped a nervous rhythm on the wooden floor.

Near the windows, Gail, Patricia, and Margie huddled together, their heads bowed. Margie's brother, Eddie, leaned forward, his elbows resting on his knees as he scanned the room. Shannon sat a row behind them with Melissa, her hands clasped in silent prayer. Melissa's young granddaughter tugged at her sleeve, her wide eyes darting nervously around the room. The girl clutched a small stuffed bear, its fur worn and patched, to her chest.

Micky Vermooch stood near the door, leaning casually against the wall. Snow dusted his dark coat and hat, and his sharp blue eyes scanned the congregation. Though his accent set him apart, he had become a steady presence in Bayou Vista—someone folks had come to rely on, even if they didn't fully understand him. A faint hum escaped him, something melodic and haunting, but when Loretta turned to look, he only smiled faintly. His fingers toyed with a silver ring on his left hand, the faint etching of a crescent moon catching the light.

Preacher John stepped up to the pulpit, adjusting his glasses with trembling fingers. The room grew quiet, save for the rustling of coats and the occasional sniffle. His gaze swept over the packed pews, lingering on the empty spots where familiar faces should have been. He took a deep breath, the sound amplified by the stillness. The weight of the congregation's collective grief pressed down on him, making the air feel heavier than the thick snow outside.

"Good morning, everyone," he began, his voice deep and steady. "Merry Christmas."

A murmur of responses rippled through the crowd, faint but heartfelt. Brenda whispered her response, but her voice cracked halfway through. Somewhere in the back, a baby let out a soft cry, quickly hushed by its mother.

"I know this ain't the Christmas morning we hoped for," Preacher John continued, his voice thick with emotion. "We've all been through something none of us will ever forget. And we've lost folks we care about." His voice faltered briefly, but he cleared his throat and pressed on. "But this morning, I want us to remember what Christmas is really about—light, hope, and redemption."

Brenda wiped a tear from her cheek, the faint glitter of it catching the soft glow of the candles. "Redemption," she murmured to herself, her voice almost inaudible.

The preacher glanced at her, then back to the congregation. "Last night, we faced our past, our mistakes, and our fears. And it is not easy to do that. But y'all showed courage. You stood up. And now, we gotta figure out how to move forward."

Micky straightened, his voice cutting through the silence like a knife. "Preacher's right. We've been through hell, but that doesn't mean we stay there, does it?" Heads turned toward him, drawn to his smooth English accent, a stark contrast to the Southern drawls around him. "We've got to honor what happened. And we've got to remember."

Loretta frowned, her brows knitting together. "How're we supposed to do that, Micky? Light a candle and say a prayer? That ain't going to bring back the ones we lost."

"No, love," Micky said gently. "It won't. But we can make sure their names ain't forgotten. Every year, we gather. At the tree in the square. We leave something—a gift, a memory, a token. Something to remind us of them and what we learned."

Firecracker scoffed, her arms still crossed. "And what's that going to do, huh? Fix everything? Make us all feel better?"

"No," Micky said, his gaze steady. "But it'll keep us honest. The marsh doesn't forget, love. And neither should we."

The room buzzed with murmurs. Jason rubbed his chin thoughtfully. "I reckon it's a good idea," he said. "Better than just pretending none of this happened."

"Exactly," Taylor chimed in from her spot near the back. Her soft drawl carried just enough weight to turn a few heads. "We owe Mary Ellen that much. And everyone else, too."

Brenda nodded, her voice soft but firm. "I think it's beautiful. A way to remember without letting the past eat us alive."

Eddie leaned back, his arms crossed. "What if folks don't want to remember? What if they just want to move on?"

Cindy Blevins turned to him, her voice trembling but steady. "We don't have a choice, Eddie. If we don't remember, the marsh will make sure we do."

A hush fell over the room. Everyone knew the truth in Cindy's words. The marsh had its own way of keeping people accountable, and last night had proved that in ways no one could deny.

Preacher John raised his hands, his expression resolute. "Let's make it official, then. A new tradition for Bayou Vista. Every Christmas, we honor those we've lost and the lessons we've learned."

Melissa smiled faintly. "A Christmas tradition," she said, her voice barely above a whisper. "That's something I can get behind."

"Me too," Shannon added, her voice steady. "It's the least we can do."

Preacher John nodded, his expression firm. "Then let's pray, y'all. For Mary Ellen. For those we've lost. And for the strength to keep their memory alive."

The congregation bowed their heads, the room silent except for the preacher's voice. It rose steady and sure, carrying their prayers through the stillness. Snow tapped softly against the windows, the sound almost like a rhythm to the preacher's words.

As the prayer ended, a sudden gust of wind swept through the church, extinguishing half the candles on the altar. The congregation gasped, their heads snapping up as the shadows deepened. Micky's eyes narrowed, his lips pressing into a thin line.

Outside, the Christmas tree lights in the square flickered once, twice, and then glowed brighter than before, casting a strange, golden hue across the snow. From the edge of the marsh, a low hum began, faint but growing louder, like the echo of voices long forgotten.

Tina clutched her Bible tighter. "What was that?" she whispered.

Micky stepped forward, his boots echoing on the wooden floor. "The marsh," he said softly, his voice carrying an edge of unease.

As the townsfolk spilled into the streets, their steps faltered, their whispers hurried and uncertain. They avoided glancing toward the horizon where the marsh lay far beyond the town, its unseen presence still palpable. Above them, the sun broke through the clouds, but the light felt colder than before. And though the marsh was distant, the faint hum of something unnatural lingered in their minds, a reminder that peace would not come without a price.

~ 34 ~

THE DAY AFTER...

The following day, *Bayou Bliss Coffee House* was back to its usual hum. The bell above the door jingled as folks came in, stomping snow from their boots and rubbing their gloved hands together. The smell of chicory coffee and warm beignets filled the air, mingling with the sound of chairs scraping on the wooden floor and the low murmur of conversations. Outside, the fresh snow shimmered under the pale sunlight, casting a rare glow over Bayou Vista.

Gail was the first to arrive, bundled in her thick coat with a bright red scarf wrapped snugly around her neck. She carried herself like a woman who'd seen the worst of times but still believed in the best of people. Patricia trailed in behind her, shaking snow off her boots.

"You're late," Gail teased as they found a table near the window. "Snow didn't stop me none."

"Late?" Patricia rolled her eyes. "I was up before the sun, Gail. You know it takes longer when you've got grandkids hanging off your legs."

The two laughed as Brenda Menifee appeared from behind the counter, carrying a fresh pot of coffee. She wore her usual red and black apron, the color popping against the muted winter tones outside. "Morning, ladies. Coffee's fresh, and the beignets are about as good as they get this side of heaven."

Brenda poured their coffee as the bell jingled again. This time, it was Loretta, Tricia, and Taylor. The three of them looked tired but calm, as if the weight of the night before had settled into something they could carry—at least for now.

"Morning, y'all," Brenda greeted, motioning to the table beside Gail and Patricia's. "Grab a seat. I'll bring over the good stuff."

"Morning," Loretta mumbled, plopping into a chair. Taylor gave her a sympathetic pat on the shoulder before sitting down herself.

"Where's Rosie?" Gail asked, glancing toward the door.

"Probably still sleeping," Patricia replied. "She had a lot to say last night at the diner. Took it out of her, I reckon."

The bell jingled again, and in walked Sheriff Emmett, his hat dusted with snow. He greeted the room with a slight nod before heading straight for the counter. "Brenda, you got something strong? It's been a long couple of days."

Brenda chuckled. "Coffee's strong, Sheriff. That do?"

"That'll do," Emmett said, tipping his hat. He turned to see Micky Vermooch walking in, his long coat trailing snowflakes onto the floor. Micky nodded at him as he headed toward a table near the back, his movements slow and deliberate.

"Cold out there, isn't it?" Micky said, his English accent lilting in the cozy room.

"Colder than we're used to," Brenda replied, pouring him a cup of coffee. "Y'all don't feel this in England?"

Micky smiled faintly. "Not quite like this, love. Louisiana's got its own way of doing things, even with the weather."

By mid-morning, the coffee house was nearly full. Rosie finally stumbled in, bundled in an oversized coat and looking like she hadn't slept much. She waved half-heartedly before grabbing a chair next to Gertie, who was already sipping her coffee and looking as sharp as ever.

"Y'all hear about Shannon?" Gertie said, leaning forward conspiratorially. "She left that little hourglass by the tree."

"I saw that," Patricia said. "Thought it was beautiful. Time's something we can't get back, you know."

Taylor nodded. "It felt like everyone left a piece of themselves there. Did you see Firecracker with that notebook? What do you think is inside?"

Rosie snorted. "Probably some of that mess she's always hollerin' about in the store. Still, it was nice. I didn't think Firecracker had it in her."

"I think last night brought out something in all of us," Loretta said softly. "Made us all think about what we're leaving behind."

The table fell silent for a moment, the weight of her words settling over them like the snow outside. Then Brenda broke the tension, setting a fresh tray of beignets in the center of the table.

"Y'all hush and eat. You can't have deep thoughts on an empty stomach."

A cold draft slipped through the coffee house, making Loretta shiver. She pulled her coat tighter around her shoulders and glanced toward the window. Outside, the square was quiet, the Christmas tree still standing proud in its center. The tokens left the night before glinted faintly in the sunlight—the small hourglass, the wooden cross, and the old key hanging from a low branch. Each item seemed to carry its own story, and together, they gave the tree an almost sacred quality.

"You feel that?" Loretta asked, her voice barely above a whisper. "It's colder now than it was earlier."

"It's just the wind," Patricia said quickly, though her voice had an edge to it. She avoided looking at the window, instead busying herself with her coffee. "This old place's got cracks everywhere."

Gail frowned but didn't say anything. She, too, had felt the chill. It wasn't the kind of cold that came from snow; it was deeper, sharper, and it left an ache in its wake.

In the corner, Sheriff Emmett sat across from Micky, the two of them speaking quietly. Micky's blue eyes flicked toward the window as Emmett leaned forward.

"You reckon it's over?" Emmett asked, his voice low.

Micky didn't answer right away. He took a slow sip of coffee, his gaze distant. "Depends on the town," he said finally. "Depends on whether you lot remember what you learned."

Emmett frowned. "You make it sound like a test."

"Everything's a test, Sheriff," Micky said, his voice steady. "Whether you pass or fail depends on whether you're paying attention."

The Sheriff leaned back, his hand on the coffee cup. "You sure have a way of making a man think, Micky."

Micky smiled faintly. "That's the idea."

As the morning wore on, the conversations ebbed and flowed. People came and went, their spirits a little lighter than they'd been the day before. Outside, the square looked like something out of a Christmas card. The Christmas tree in the center still stood tall, its branches adorned with the tokens left the night before. The faint glow of its lights seemed softer now, almost reverent.

Loretta watched the tree from the window, her chin resting on her hand. "Think she'd be happy?" she asked quietly.

Gail, sitting beside her, glanced out at the square. "I think she'd want you to be happy," she said. "And I think she'd want us to do better."

Loretta nodded, her eyes misting over. "I promised her. At the tree, I promised her I'd do better."

"And you will," Gail said firmly. "You've got a good heart, Loretta. Don't you ever doubt that."

As noon approached, Micky stood, pulling his coat tight around him. He left a few bills on the table and tipped his hat toward Brenda. "Thanks for the coffee, love."

"You heading out already?" she asked.

"Things to see, people to talk to," he replied with a faint smile. "You know how it is."

As he stepped outside, the cold air hit him, but he didn't seem to notice. His boots crunched in the snow as he walked toward the square. He paused at the Christmas tree, brushing snow off a low branch. The key left by Cindy caught the light, its metallic surface gleaming faintly. Micky ran his fingers over the branch before stepping back, his gaze lingering.

For a moment, he stood there, silent and still, as if listening to something no one else could hear. The wind picked up slightly, carrying with it a faint, almost imperceptible hum. Micky tilted his head, his expression unreadable.

Then, without a word, he turned and disappeared down the road, his figure fading into the snowy horizon.

Back inside, the warmth of *Bayou Bliss* enveloped the remaining townsfolk. The hum of voices and the clatter of cups filled the air, a comforting reminder that life went on, even after the hardest nights.

As Brenda refilled cups and wiped down tables, she glanced toward the window. The snow had started falling again, soft flakes that danced in the wind. The Christmas tree in the square stood tall and proud, its branches heavy with memories, a symbol of the promises they'd made.

And in the distance, far beyond the town, the marsh lay quiet—watching, waiting.

~ 35 ~

A LEGACY REMEMBERED

Years had passed, but the memory of that fateful Christmas Eve still lingered in Bayou Vista like a low-hanging fog. The marsh, dark and brooding at the edge of town, stayed as quiet as ever, but it was a silence that felt alive—watching, waiting, never forgotten. Folks in Bayou Vista didn't talk about it much anymore, but they didn't need to. Every year, the town came together to decorate the Christmas tree in the square, each branch heavy with tokens left by those who refused to let the past slip away.

It wasn't just a tradition. It was a promise, one passed down from generation to generation: *Never forget.*

Late one December evening, the kind of snow folks in Bayou Vista hadn't seen in years began to fall. Big, fluffy flakes drifted from the sky, covering the rooftops, the trees, and the narrow streets. It clung to the marsh reeds and blanketed *Preacher's Pond* in a layer of pure, untouched white.

The square, as always, was the heart of the town. Families bustled around, kids bundled up in mismatched scarves and mittens, their laughter ringing out as they tossed snowballs and tried to build lopsided snowmen. The Christmas tree stood tall in the center, its lights twinkling in the fading daylight. The tokens from years past glinted faintly among the branches—small wooden carvings, faded photographs, a rusted key, and a worn hourglass. Each item told a story, a piece of the town's shared history.

Among the children playing in the square was Maggie Boudreaux, an eight-year-old with wide, curious eyes and a knack for wandering off when no one was watching. Her grandmother, Eunice, sat on a bench nearby, wrapped in her old patchwork quilt, her watchful eyes never straying far from Maggie.

"Maggie, don't you go too far now!" Eunice called, her voice carrying over the chatter. "You hear me? Snow or not, the marsh ain't no place for a child."

"I won't, Granny!" Maggie called back, her boots crunching through the snow as she drifted toward the edge of the square, where Preacher's Pond lay still and quiet.

Maggie stopped just short of the pond. The air was colder here, and the snow seemed thicker, muffling every sound. Something caught her eye—a glint of silver poking out from beneath the snow. Kneeling down, she brushed the snow away with her mittened hands, revealing a weathered photograph.

She held it up carefully, her breath visible in the crisp air. The picture was old, the edges frayed and worn. It showed a young girl standing near the marsh, her red hair tied back with a ribbon, her dress plain but neat. The faint letters "M.E." were scrawled on the back in a delicate hand.

Maggie's chest tightened as she stared at the girl's face. There was something in her eyes—something that felt sad and knowing all at once. Maggie couldn't look away.

A chill ran down Maggie's spine, and she turned toward the marsh. Just beyond the line of trees, a figure stood cloaked in shadow, still as a statue. They held a lantern, its light steady and warm against the growing darkness. Maggie's heart raced, but it wasn't fear she felt. It was something deeper, something that made her feel as though she were being seen for the first time.

The figure raised the lantern slightly, the light flickering for just a moment before it steadied again. Maggie blinked, and the figure was gone, the marsh silent once more.

"Maggie!" Eunice's voice cut through the stillness. "What are you doin' over there, child? You'll catch your death in this cold!"

Maggie stood, tucking the photograph into her coat pocket as she hurried back to her grandmother's side.

Eunice dusted the snow off Maggie's coat, her expression a mix of relief and exasperation. "What'd I tell you about wanderin'? The marsh ain't no place for a little girl, no matter how curious you get."

"I found something, Granny," Maggie said, pulling the photograph from her pocket. "Do you know who she is?"

Eunice froze, her breath catching as she took the photograph from Maggie's hands. Her fingers trembled as she traced the edges of the picture. "Mary Ellen," she whispered, her voice thick with emotion. "It's her."

"Who's Mary Ellen?" Maggie asked, her wide eyes full of curiosity.

Eunice sighed, tucking the photograph back into Maggie's coat. "She's the reason we do what we do every Christmas. She's the one the marsh took."

Maggie frowned. "Why'd the marsh take her?"

"It ain't that simple," Eunice said, pulling Maggie close. "We forgot her when she needed us most. We turned away when we should've stood by her. And the marsh... well, it don't take kindly to folks who forget."

As Eunice spoke, others began to gather around, their voices low as they noticed the photograph in Maggie's hand.

"That's Mary Ellen," a lady said softly, her breath fogging in the cold air. "She was just a girl."

"Just a girl," another lady echoed, her voice tinged with regret. "But we let her down."

That night, as the snow continued to fall, the town gathered in the square. The Christmas tree stood at the center, its lights casting a soft glow over the crowd. Children clung to their parents' hands, their laughter replaced by the quiet reverence of the moment.

The Preacher stood near the base of the tree, his Bible tucked under his arm. He cleared his throat, his voice steady despite the emotion that weighed heavily in the air. "We come together tonight to remember Mary Ellen," he began. "And to honor the promise we made—to never forget what happens when we turn away from those who need us."

One by one, the townsfolk stepped forward, leaving tokens at the base of the tree. A small carved bird, a delicate lace ribbon, a handful of dried flowers—each item was placed with care, a silent pledge to keep the memory alive.

Maggie approached the tree with Eunice by her side, the photograph clutched in her small hands. She knelt carefully, brushing the snow away from the base of the tree before placing the picture among the other tokens. For a moment, she hesitated, her eyes searching the branches above.

"Think she knows, Granny?" she asked, her voice barely audible.

Eunice knelt beside her, placing a hand on her shoulder. "She knows, Maggie. She knows we're tryin' to do right by her."

As the square emptied, a faint whisper carried through the air, soft and fleeting. It moved like the snow, barely noticeable but impossible to ignore.

"Remember me."

The townsfolk paused, some glancing toward the marsh, others clutching their coats tighter. Maggie turned to Eunice, her eyes wide. "Did you hear that, Granny?"

Eunice nodded slowly, her expression unreadable. "I heard it, baby. I heard it."

The Christmas tree in the square grew taller with each passing year, its branches heavy with memories. The tokens left behind told the story of a town that had learned to remember, not just for Mary Ellen, but for everyone who had been forgotten.

And on nights when the snow fell and the wind carried whispers from the marsh, the people of Bayou Vista listened. They remembered.

And the Watcher watched, her lantern glowing softly in the distance—a silent guardian, a reminder, a promise.

D*ear Readers,*

Thank you for choosing to read The Watcher! I hope you enjoyed the journey as much as I loved bringing it to life. If you'd like to stay updated on all my upcoming releases or even have the chance to become a character in one of my stories, be sure to follow my Facebook page. I truly enjoy connecting with my readers and hearing your thoughts, so feel free to reach out and say hello!

facebook.com/AuthorCarolACampbellGhostStories

or you can email me:
authorcarola.campbell@hotmail.com

I hope you enjoyed The Watcher as much as I loved writing it! If the story resonated with you, I'd be truly grateful if you could take a moment to leave a review. Your thoughts mean the world to me, and your support helps other readers discover my books. Thank you for being part of this journey, and I can't wait to hear what you think!

Thanks!
Carol

www.ingramcontent.com/pod-product-compliance
Lightning Source LLC
Chambersburg PA
CBHW020322160726
47992CB00004B/1655